A LIFE FOR A DEATH is by John
Creasey writing as Gordon Ashe of
which there are now over forty titles
and many have been published by
Corgi Books.
Born in 1908, John Creasey died in June
1973. Overall, his books have sold
nearly a hundred million copies and
have been translated into 28 languages.
As well as travelling extensively, he had
a particular interest in politics and was
the founder of *All Party Alliance*,
which advocates a new system of
government by the best candidates
from all parties and independents. He
fought in five parliamentary by-elections
for the movement.

Also by John Creasey

and published by Corgi Books

John Creasey
writing as
Gordon Ashe

A Life for a Death

CORGI BOOKS
A DIVISION OF TRANSWORLD PUBLISHERS LTD

A LIFE FOR A DEATH

A CORGI BOOK 0 552 09676 8

Originally published in Great Britain
by John Long Ltd.

PRINTING HISTORY
John Long edition published 1973
Corgi edition published 1975

Corgi Books are published by Transworld Publishers Ltd.,
Cavendish House, 57–59 Uxbridge Road, London, W.5
Made and printed in Great Britain by
Cox & Wyman Ltd., London, Reading and Fakenham

Contents

CHAPTER ONE

THE QUARRY

'THERE he is,' said the slightly built, clean-shaven youth.

'Where?' demanded his companion, who was thicker set, and had a curly dark beard and sideburns which made him, somehow, look younger than his years.

'With that group,' the first man said, but he was careful not to point.

'The five men?'

'Yes. He is the big one.'

'My,' exclaimed the man with the beard, 'he is a real giant of a man!'

'He is all that,' agreed the clean-shaven man.

'Why do they want him dead?'

'You will be in trouble if you become too curious,' said the first man. 'And never forget that walls have ears.'

They fell silent as they watched.

They were at the top of the Spanish Steps in Rome, near the flower-sellers who sat or squatted with their huge baskets filled with mimosa and bougainvillaea and canna, as well as smaller, brilliant-hued flowers which were shaded from the sun by huge umbrellas. Tourists, even in this season of early spring, were thick on the steps, some standing and looking down, like the two men by the stone wall. Others were sauntering up and down, a few hurrying; and these, obviously, were not tourists but Romans going about their business. There were the photographers and the sellers of postcards and souvenirs, of newspapers, magazines and books.

The two young men – both Italians – continued to watch the group of five, which suddenly became animated. There was some cheek-kissing and hugging, much handshaking, many expressions of good wishes, and obvious farewells. Then the five

7

broke up, three coming upwards, two going down. In the middle of those coming up was the 'real giant of a man'. He walked with the casual ease of the very fit human being. He was truly huge, at least a head taller than his tallest companion. In contrast to his corn-coloured hair, each of the others was very dark, one clearly Italian, the other, more portly, almost certainly French.

'It is so easy,' the bearded young Italian said. 'One bullet between the eyes is enough.'

'A bullet for a blond beast.' The other laughed. 'Why not right now?'

'I am thinking about it.'

'Don't think too long,' the other urged.

Both of them waited, hidden by a huge striped umbrella. Footsteps sounded, some slow and deliberate, some sharp and hurried: men's footsteps and a woman's. The woman was almost on a level with the big man on the steps. With his two companions he was coming up with deliberate tread, obviously unworried by the bright noon-day sun. The Italian and the Frenchman – indeed most of the people on the steps – wore straw or raffia hats, floppy linen hats, many white and some gaily floral. The woman who walked quickly past the trio wore a floppy one with huge yellow daisies on it; or were they sunflowers? She did not glance right or left and she did not seem to speak, yet out of the corner of her mouth she said:

'Be careful.'

She hurried past, wearing a mini-skirt surely designed from the beginning for such legs of shapely beauty.

'So they are here,' the big man observed.

'Pat, don't take any risks.' The Italian's voice was urgent in warning. He was the host, here; the woman, one of his agents who had been sent to watch the Spanish Steps.

'Must take some risks,' the man named Pat replied; his other name was Dawlish. He did not appear to look up, but in fact he did; and he caught a glimpse of two men by the side of the umbrella. 'After all, until they shoot we won't know whether they are the men we're after. You watch them, Henri. If they look like shooting, push me away.'

'Push you? It would be like pushing a mountain!'

The big man laughed and his white teeth showed.

Another attractive, mini-skirted woman came downwards, wearing a raffia hat tilted to one side, escorted by a man twice her age, beautifully dressed in a linen suit of pale blue. She looked at Dawlish with undisguised admiration. Not only his size was impressive: his handsomeness was equally so, and was somehow enhanced by his broken nose. He had well-shaped lips and a square, cleft chin, and his face might almost have been carved out of marble by Michelangelo himself. The sun made his face so very vivid.

So did his laugh.

'Now!' breathed the bearded assassin.

'You go to the car.'

'I cannot miss this,' the bearded man said. 'It is almost a pity to kill him.'

'I tell you, go and start the car engine.'

Slowly, reluctantly, the man with the beard moved towards a little white Fiat, of a colour and shape as common here as were Volkswagens in Germany and Morris Minors in England. The clean-shaven man edged closer to the shade of the huge umbrella, hidden by it, and drew his right hand from the pocket of his jacket.

The girl with the floppy hat reached the top of the steps. She was hidden from him by the umbrellas and the flowers and the flower-sellers and a little group of customers, all welcome because they were distracting attention from him.

His pistol was air-powered, and would make only a sharp *zutt*! of sound.

He raised it, as Dawlish neared the top, well within range. He pointed it at Dawlish's forehead, right between the eyes.

The girl appeared, behind him.

The man on Dawlish's right slipped and cannoned into Dawlish as the shot was fired. There was hardly a sound at all, and a passing car drowned what there was, and the bullet missed. For a chagrined second the man stood and watched as Dawlish and the others recovered their balance. Dawlish still smiled, as if he hadn't the faintest idea that he had been within an ace of death.

Then the girl with the floppy hat appeared from behind the gay umbrella and confronted the assassin as he spun round. No one else was close by her in those crucial seconds, and the umbrella hid not only the flower-seller but the people at the top of the steps.

There was a split second of recognition; instant, appalled. Then the man levelled the pistol and shot her between the eyes.

The expression on her face on the instant she realized what was going to happen was of stupefaction. Fear chased it across her eyes, as she had no chance at all to dodge aside, time only to open her lips to cry out in anguish; but the bullet struck before she had uttered a sound, and fear died with death, taking away all expression with it.

The only witness was the bearded man, a few yards away, standing by the Fiat. The assassin took the dead girl by the wrist and pulled her towards him, then with a deft twist made her fall so that most of her body was huddled up behind the great umbrella. All that showed were her beautiful slim legs. He snatched at an open box of mimosa and covered her legs with the tiny yellow blooms, then walked steadily towards the car. As he did so he glanced to the right.

The big man was at the top of the steps.

The engine of the Fiat raced.

The clean-shaven assassin rushed towards it, far enough away from Dawlish to reach the car and scramble in. The car raced off, engine now roaring, but only Dawlish took the slightest notice, for noisy engines were part of the life of Rome.

Dawlish leapt forward.

There would have been a chance, if a slender one, of his stopping the Fiat, but a dozen people came hurrying, obviously a sightseeing party agog and looking over the wall towards the foot of the steps and the Piazza di Spagna beyond. The car went at a furious roar, and a woman jumped out of its path. The brakes of another car squealed. There was just space and time for Dawlish to rush in pursuit from the top of the steps, and he was big and powerful enough to push the Fiat to one side, for it was travelling very slowly, not yet far from the row of umbrellas.

Dawlish sprang forward.

As he did so, a bullet from someone among the crowd of

tourists struck him on the side of the head, and he went down with awful suddenness. A woman cried out and an Englishman exclaimed: 'What the hell!' as Dawlish fell against the umbrella which half-concealed the dead girl, scattering boxes and crates and flowers and flower-sellers, photographs and postcard-sellers and their postcards, and sightseers too; and the crimson of his blood merged with the red stripes of the great umbrella, so that no one noticed it at first.

When the Italian and the French policemen who had been with Dawlish arrived at the spot a crowd of fifty or sixty people had gathered, a policeman in his dark winter uniform was pushing his way through and the protests of the flower-sellers died on their lips as they saw the huge man who lay there so still.

Now a mile away, the Fiat was travelling along the road towards the heart of the city, no faster and no slower than the traffic, anonymous because there was so many models, exactly the same.

Close by the steps one of the crowd, the sightseer who had shot Dawlish, was unsuspected. The guide, at first stunned, gradually pulled himself together and shepherded his crowd.

'Please come with me,' he called. 'We shall be late. It would obviously be a tragedy to be late.' He pushed a man here, pulled a woman there, pleaded and counted: '...nine, ten, eleven. Please come.'

Among those he pulled was the man who had fired the shot, and this man, thin, clean-shaven, with a crew-cut and wearing horn-rimmed glasses, allowed himself to be herded like the rest of the party while the guide pitched his voice high, calling out the name of his tour, pleading and beguiling and informing. 'Believe me or not, there are one hundred and thirty-six steps to go downwards, one hundred thirty-seven to go up! ... No, signor, not today you try, there is no time! ... The idea it was French to have the Spanish Steps in Italy, how funny please ... There you see the shop Number 31, that is where John Keats in 1821 killed himself, we go soon to see him in ze death-mask. ...'

He reached the piazza with all of his party. No one on the steps seemed to have any idea what had happened above, but those at the top saw a police car arrive, and an ambulance immediately afterwards. Those who took the trouble saw the bandage he wrapped about Dawlish's head after the wound had been padded to stop the bleeding, and watched as if mesmerized as two men, not much more than half Dawlish's size, took him by the ankles and by the shoulders and lifted him on to the stretcher and slid him into the ambulance.

The French police chief and the Italian police chief climbed in with him, the Italian speaking briskly over the radio, giving a description of the two men in the Fiat, quite unaware that the killer was now in the piazza, gaping at the English tea shop nearby.

Suddenly a man called out: 'My God, look at that girl!'

As the crowd peered at him and he stared down, an elaborately uniformed carabiniere thrust himself forward. He was the second man to see the lovely legs almost hidden by the bloom of mimosa, like a shroud of furry yellow pearls. He pulled mimosa away and was the first to see the bullet hole in the girl's forehead, and the blue ridge about the edge of the hole and the seepage of blood.

'Another one!' he gasped. 'One more is dead.'

And the crowd surged forward to see what new horror lay before them.

Even before the ambulance reached the St. Josepha Hospital, news was flashing round the world by radio and television, teleprint and telephoto. 'Dawlish is dead.' To the man in the street this meant nothing at first, but to policemen everywhere it brought a chill of horror. So it did to newspaper and television and radio newsmen wherever they were.

'Dawlish is dead!'

'My God! *Dawlish* is dead.'

'Dawlish is dead, Dawlish is dead, Dawlish is dead.'

Soon, newspapers in Italy and France, England and America, Japan and Germany, throughout the whole Western world, carried the story. At first it appeared in small print in the stop-press columns, then it drew single-column headlines, soon it was bannered across the front pages, driving off political stories and stories of great disasters and sex sensations. The headlines were varied, now:

Dawlish is Dead
World's Number 1 Policeman Murdered
World's Top Cop Dies by Assassin's Bullet
Patrick Dawlish, Greatest Policeman – Dies of Wounds

Soon the best newspapermen in the world began to present more details: of how he was shot and why he was so highly regarded. One told the story in a few sentences:

Patrick Dawlish, leader of the Crime Haters, the Englishman who did more than anyone else to organize the fight against crime throughout the world, died of an assassin's bullet at the top of Rome's Spanish Steps at the very moment of his greatest personal triumph. Dawlish, Deputy Assistant Commissioner for Crime at London's New Scotland Yard, the man who was once the most daring secret-service agent and lone-wolf crime fighter, had just been elected permanent head of the organization known as the World's Crime Conference – the most powerful crime-fighting force in existence.

Every nation with a police force, which means every nation in the world, was represented at the conference, from Russia to Malawi, from the United States to Peru. Every delegate voted for Dawlish as permanent head. Without a single exception. Every delegate gave him a standing ovation after his election, another after his brief speech of acceptance.

He gave hope and faith to the world's police.

He did more to fight world crime – which means crime on everyone's doorstep – than any other individual.

His death is not simply a tragedy. It is a disaster.

This story, elaborated with more and more detail, was syndicated first throughout the United States, then throughout the West, almost as quickly – in its essence – throughout the world beyond the Iron Curtain, as well as Africa, India, China; the lands of the Arabs and the land of the Jews.

It spread everywhere within a few hours of it being written, and the one statement which was never altered was the very last statement of all:

His death is not simply a tragedy. It is a disaster.

While the story spread and pictures of Dawlish were flashed on screens and on front pages and the Italian police searched for the men in the Fiat, another almost equally desperate search was going on, not for a criminal but for Dawlish's wife. She was known to be travelling in the North of England, for her mother lived in Scotland and she was on her way to see the older woman. But she had gone off the beaten track in her own tiny car, a Morris Minor. She was known to love isolated spots and to stay at remote farmhouses, often anonymously and using her maiden name of Deverall, because she did not want the inevitable publicity and attention that her married name drew. On that particular day no one knew for certain where she was, yet her friends among London society were desperately anxious that she should be told privately, not run into the dread news by chance on a television screen or a front page. No one could imagine what the effect on her would be if quite out of the blue she saw her husband's photograph and the official report of his death.

In fact, Dawlish was not dead.

He was hovering on the brink. Rome's most renowned brain surgeon was operating on him. And at the same time the governing committee of the Crime Haters was in the hotel where the convention had just been held, debating the situation.

CHAPTER TWO

THE OFFICIAL REPORT

GENERAL SALVATORI, the supreme commander of the Guardie de Finanza with his headquarters in Rome, was one of the men who had been with Dawlish on the Spanish Steps. He had been in the Guardie since the end of the war and was not only its delegate in the world Police Convention but was also the liaison officer between the Guardie de Finanza – which, apart from protecting Italy's frontiers from smuggling, also dealt with most offences dealing with money and finance – the Guardie di Pubblica Sicurezza, and with the Corps di Carabinieri. Thus Salvatori represented the three main police forces of Italy within the Crime Haters.

A lean, bright-eyed, dark-haired man, he was almost revered in Italy. When he had first encouraged representation at the conference Italian participation had been virtually assured. He had been the chairman of the session just finished: it was the custom for the chief delegate of the host country to take the chair at all conference sessions. It was on Salvatori's orders that the official note of Dawlish's death had been sent out; and the only man present at the governing committee who knew that the report was not true was M. le Deputy Directeur of the Prefecture of Police in Paris. Like Dawlish, he had been brought into the police service because of his extensive knowledge of world affairs and of world crime and criminals. At the conference he represented the uniformed police of Paris, the Criminal Investigation Department or the Sûreté Nationale and the Intelligence Service. He was actually the leader of the Police Judiciare, the equivalent of London's Criminal Investigation Department. He had known Dawlish for some twenty years, but had come as delegate because of the retirement of one and the death of another earlier delegate from France.

His name was Henri Pierre-Jacques. He was plump, pale, rather prone to breathlessness, and his sharp features and very alert eyes were alike concealed by his puffy cheeks.

These two men, with tall, rangy Commyns of the Chicago Police Department and Fernandez Lohn of Brazil, were the members of the governing committee, with Dawlish their chairman. Lohn had been recalled to Brazil because of the assassination of the Army Chief of Staff; so Salvatori, Pierre-Jacques and Commyns were the only three who gathered in the suite at the great new hotel, which overlooked the walls of the city in one way and over the Via Appia in the other; there were glimpses of the Colosseum and, between trees and tall buildings, of the River Tiber. From here, gilded by the evening sun, the river looked more like liquid gold than muddy water.

The three men sat round a table with a variety of bottles at their sides: whisky, soda, gin, Dubonnet, Campari, sherry, brandy, vodka and rum. They all had long drinks, and sipped slowly. Salvatori smoked long, thin, brown cigarettes; Pierre-Jacques did not smoke, yet seemed to have a continual smoker's cough; Commyns, who had not only a long, lean look but a very tanned face, did not smoke or cough. His blue eyes often held a twinkle. He looked as if he should be wearing a Stetson and seemed to carry an aura of the open spaces.

He said, neither approving nor disapproving: 'So you spread the report that Pat was dead?'

'I did just that,' replied Salvatori, whose English had a slight American accent.

'You must have had a good reason,' Commyns remarked.

'I think it is very good,' replied Salvatori.

'So do I,' Pierre-Jacques put in.

'What is it?' asked Commyns, as if he would need a lot of convincing.

'Neil,' said Salvatori, 'you were not here in time to talk to Patrick before the meetings. We had planned to discuss the situation here this evening.' When Commyns made no comment the Italian went on: 'His life has been in danger for the past three months. Three attempts have been made to kill him. One of my agents received information that another attempt would be made today. That is why we both went with him. We hoped – we expected – to catch his assailants. But' – he raised his hands in a helpless gesture – 'they were too clever for us.'

'Why didn't we all know about this before?' demanded Commyns.

'He did not tell us,' remarked Pierre-Jacques.

'If he'd told us perhaps he wouldn't be at death's door right now,' Commyns said, quite sharply. He looked intently at both men, as if he was wary, even suspicious, of them. 'He *is* at death's door, isn't he? It isn't all spoof, is it?'

For a moment the other two were silent. At last, and very slowly, Salvatori placed a slip of paper in front of the American, who glanced down at a note typewritten in Italian but with a handwritten translation at the foot. The translation read:

P. D. is now in his fourth hour of surgery. Three surgeons

are in attendance and Horster from Berlin has been called in. He should be at the hospital by half past six. The patient's condition is extremely precarious.

Commyns handed the slip back with a laconic 'Thanks'.

'So it is obvious that he might die,' Pierre-Jacques said. 'If he does . . .' He broke off.

'A disaster,' declared Salvatori.

'What makes you say that?' demanded Commyns. 'What makes one man so important?' When neither of the others answered at once he went on in a matter-of-fact voice: 'So you really think Dawlish is the best detective in the world?'

Salvatori was frowning; Pierre-Jacques' eyes seemed to recede deeper into those fleshy sockets.

'No,' Salvatori answered. 'I do not think that.'

'Or the bravest?' Commyns demanded before the other could add more.

'There are many brave policemen,' remarked Pierre-Jacques.

'Or the most experienced?' demanded Commyns.

'No,' conceded Salvatori, and Pierre-Jacques said:

'I have been in the Sûreté Nationale for twenty years longer than Dawlish has been in the Metropolitan Police force of London. Many hundreds, *thousands*, of policemen have had more experience.'

'So,' said Commyns, pushing his chair back from the table, his manner wary and even defensive, 'What makes Dawlish's death, or serious injury, such a disaster? A tragedy, yes, but a disaster . . .' He left the words hanging in the air.

He had been prepared for a sharp and possibly angry reaction: all that happened was that the other two exchanged glances. Pierre-Jacques gave a little shrug and Salvatori put a match to his dead cigarette. It was very quiet in this room of golds and purples; of casts of long-dead Caesars and prints of a long-ruined Rome. The windows were closed. There was a slight hum from the air-conditioning and a distant murmur of cars from outside. The loudest sound was Pierre-Jacques' wheezy breathing. When he broke into a paroxysm of coughing it was like a barrage.

Only a few miles away, in the great hospital, brilliant surgeons fought for the life of the man who was being discussed in that room where past and present splendours met. And each of them, as well as the two anaesthetists and the nurse in attendance, knew that even if he lived the man lying there could suffer such brain damage that he might never be able to think clearly again.

'Neil,' said Salvatori, 'you were at the main session of the conference this morning.'

'Yes.'

'Didn't you feel the influence of Patrick Dawlish?'

'He was great,' Commyns conceded, simply.

'So.'

'A man can be a fine speaker but that doesn't make him indispensable,' Commyns objected. 'You lose a king and a new king takes over. You lose a president and a new president takes over. A great corporation like General Motors, say, or Dupont, loses a brilliant president and another takes over. Nothing ever stops.' When he fell silent, and neither of the others replied, he looked nettled, stood up, and went to the window and motioned towards the ruins of the Appian Way. 'A Caesar died, often by violence, and another took over. Just like that.'

'And in the end,' Salvatori said, 'there was disaster.'

'Neil . . .' began Pierre-Jacques, only to break off.

'Neil,' repeated Salvatori, 'you have not known Patrick Dawlish for very long.'

'I've known him long enough to be sure he's a great guy,' Commyns insisted.

'But not the only one,' Pierre-Jacques remarked.

'That's exactly what I mean. He's not the only great policeman or detective. No organization can run on one man.'

'No,' agreed Salvatori, slowly. He placed his cigarette on a an ashtray which bore the head of a centurion, and leaned back in his chair.

'Let me say this.' Commyns spoke more quickly than usual. 'I like Pat Dawlish. I have a tremendous admiration for him. I was all for him this morning. Even if there had been someone else to vote for I would have voted for Patrick. But I don't feel any sense of godship about the man, and some of you seem to.'

'Neil,' began Salvatori, as if very anxious to start afresh, 'there is no one quality in Dawlish which raises him above the rest of us. He *is* above us. There is a mixture of all the qualities we have and something more, a kind of mystique . . . No, don't scoff,' he went on more sharply. 'Your President Eisenhower had it. Winston Churchill had it. They could bring people together as no one else could. Here in Europe Eisenhower did this when the people round his table planning vast military operations were all very different temperaments, skills and convictions. Dawlish has this quality where we of the police are concerned. He can bring us all together. It is not only his great courage, although *I* think perhaps he *is* the bravest man I have ever met, policeman or not. It is a quality of the spirit. However, I do not think that if he dies the whole of the organization will collapse. I do think that for a while it will be less effective. Perhaps dangerously less effective.'

'There is one hope,' put in Pierre-Jacques.

'What is that?' Salvatori asked.

'The conference might be so angry about his assassination that they could be stronger in unity than before.'

'That is possible,' conceded Salvatori, as if the thought were both new and welcome.

'You mean out of vengeance?' Commyns asked; it was not quite a derisive comment but it did not fall far short.

'Yes, exactly that,' replied Pierre-Jacques. 'You will soon find, Neil, that most of the delegates love Patrick Dawlish. It is as simple as that. But . . .' He spread his plump hands and his near-buried eyes seemed to smoulder at Commyns. 'There is something equally simple which you may more readily understand.'

'I would be very glad to hear it,' Commyns said.

'His enemies hate him,' stated Pierre-Jacques calmly. 'That is because they fear him so much. And men who hate can lose their judgment.'

Commyns opened his mouth but closed it again without speaking. He moved from the window for the first time, and his expression changed, there was no hint of doubt or decision now, only of deep interest. He pulled his chair back, then moved to the trolley with the drinks, poured himself a brandy, and, with a gesture, asked if the others wanted another drink.

Neither accepted. He sipped, then moved to his chair and sat down.

'So they hate and fear him,' he echoed. 'That's why they shot him?'

'And why they've attacked him so often before,' Salvatori said.

'He has done them more harm than any other individual,' remarked Pierre-Jacques.

'Who are "they"?' demanded Commyns.

'You may say the Mafia. You may say any criminal organization in the world, whether its members deal in drugs or money, in human flesh, in food, in any vital commodity. You know as well as I know that the world is full of men of prey, feeding off human needs and human follies. And we, the Crime Haters, have been created to fight them. They fear us, yes. Above all, they fear Dawlish.'

Commyns said almost in exasperation: 'Okay, so they fear Dawlish more than anyone else. If he had told us they were attacking him . . .'

'There was one reason why he did not,' Salvatori stated.

'Just tell me what it was.'

'He did not believe he was more important than the rest of us,' answered Salvatori. 'He did not at first believe he was being attacked because he was one of the leaders of the Crime Haters. He thought there was more likely to be some personal reason, and he tried to find out what it was. But he began to doubt, and told me of his doubts when he was driving from the airfield on Wednesday. I was with him. Hardly had he finished when our car was nearly blown up by a hand-grenade thrown from a passing car. It actually fell into our car and Dawlish picked it up and held it until he could toss it into wasteland. There it blew up, doing no harm.'

Salvatori stopped, leaving the picture etched sharply in Commyns' mind.

One car, passing the other. A bomb, lobbed in through an open window. Dawlish, picking it up and instead of hurling it as far as he could, as fast as he could, into the path of other cars, or into crowds of people, had calmly waited to choose the spot where it could do no harm.

'There was still no absolute certainty,' Salvatori went on

'The attack might have been meant for either of us, for reasons unconnected with the Crime Haters.'

'I would say it was because of the Crime Haters,' Commyns remarked, very thoughtfully.

'Indeed, so did we. We were followed by one of my cars,' went on Salvatori, 'and this car overtook the one from which the bomb had been thrown. The driver was injured and the passenger killed. The driver knew enough to tell us, under the influence of benzedrine, that they had been paid to kill Dawlish by the Farenza, which is the Italian branch of an international criminal organization at least as powerful as the Mafia. But the Farenza does not show its hand carelessly. It must have had reason to fear him very much, because now there is a great risk of open conflict with the police of the world. So . . .' Salvatori spread his hands. 'Do these things not speak for themselves?'

'Loud and clear,' agreed Commyns, without hesitation. 'Loud and clear, even to me! What happened then?'

'We were able to trace the place the assassins came from, and to plant an agent among them. The agent reported the next attempt would be very soon. So if we had doubts of how frightened they were of Dawlish we had none left. It was Dawlish who persuaded us to allow them to attack, the intention being to capture the second lot of attackers red-handed, and so give us more evidence against Farenza. Instead . . .'

Commyns said gruffly: 'You encouraged him to take the chance.'

'Yes,' Salvatori said.

'And allowed the assassins to escape?'

'No,' Salvatori denied. 'That is not so.'

'But they did escape! It is in the report.' Commyns banged a typewritten sheet which lay in front of him.

'There were two men who killed the woman, who was our agent,' Salvatori said, 'the one who had been working among the Farenza. They got away from the scene of the crime, but they were in fact followed.'

'We know where they are,' Pierre-Jacques put in with pride and dignity. 'We can pick them up at any time we wish.'

'But obviously we wish them to take us to their leaders,' Salvatori pointed out. 'There was the actual murderer, whom we do not know and who escaped among a crowd of tourists. But we do have a good lead.'

Commyns finished his drink, leaned back in his chair, looked from one to the other, and said slowly: 'I'm sorry. I'm the fool.' He shook his head in exasperation at himself. 'I certainly am the fool. Do you know of any special reason why they want Dawlish dead, except the guess that he was close to them?'

'No,' answered Salvatori slowly. 'But when the attack happened, when a man in the crowd called out: "He's dead!" and when Dawlish looked as if he were dead, then ...' He pursed his lips. 'Then I thought it would be a good thing to allow the world to think he was dead.'

'The world,' echoed Commyns, 'including the Farenza, who want him dead. Don't tell me, I can take it from there. The Farenza, believing Dawlish dead, may now take risks they wouldn't have taken when he was alive. They will feel more secure. They don't know that two of their assassins are known. They don't know how close we are to them. So for the time being it's better to allow the world to believe Dawlish is dead, as that is the only way to convince the Farenza.'

'Whether he recovers or not,' Pierre-Jacques agreed. 'Neil, do you think we did the right thing?'

'Yes,' Commyns now said without hesitation.

'Now we have to decide how best to take advantage of the situation,' declared Salvatori.

'Maybe you've arranged all this,' interrupted Commyns. 'But shouldn't we first make sure that no one will talk about the operation? When you come to the point, can you conceal the fact that the best brain surgeon in the world is on his way? That all the resources of the finest hospital in Italy are being used to try to save a life?'

'Yes,' answered Salvatori.

'How?' Commyns demanded.

'We have arranged for an extremely important member of the Italian Government to be at the hospital,' said Salvatori. 'He has in fact gone in for a tumour of the brain. All the publicity will be centred on him. Arrangements have also been made for an autopsy on the body of a man of Dawlish's size to be carried out and for the death certificate to be issued in Dawlish's name – the cause of death will officially be from a

22

bullet wound.' For the first time since the three men had met here, Salvatori smiled with some degree of satisfaction. 'Now, as you rightly say, we must decide what to do next.'

'And the first thing,' said Pierre-Jacques, 'is to decide whether to tell Dawlish's wife the truth or allow her to believe that her husband is dead.' When Commyns began to speak he went on: 'So far, only we and some of the medical staff at the hospital know the truth. The Metropolitan Police of Scotland Yard do not, and if they behave as if the story is true then the leaders of the Farenza will need little more convincing. However, they might have Dawlish's wife watched, and her behaviour could give the truth away.'

After a long pause Commyns said flatly: 'Either you put her through hell or you take the risk of spoiling the whole plot. Is that it?' After another pause he added with a wary smile: 'Some wives would be glad to know that their husbands were dead. Could Dawlish's wife be one of them?'

'No,' answered Pierre-Jacques with absolute assurance. 'I should say that the Dawlishes are as much in love with each other as when they first met, over twenty years ago.'

'I think perhaps even more,' murmured Salvatori.

CHAPTER THREE

FELICITY DAWLISH

ON the morning which followed the shooting in Rome, Felicity Dawlish did not know anything at all about it. In fact, she was as happy as she could be when on her own; and there were times when she realized that spells away from Pat contributed a great deal towards their mutual happiness. Absence could indeed make the heart grow fonder! She actually thought that as she drove her little car along a narrow road not far from Scap Fell. It was one of the clear blue days with small, high white clouds which made England's Lake District beautiful enough to catch the heart. In the far distance between the craggy hills was Derwentwater, but closer to her was a smaller lake, now a vivid blue, reflecting the rocks of a sheer wall on the far side and, suddenly, mirrored the yellow of a bank of daffodils which were hidden from direct view by jutting rocks.

She caught her breath, got out of the car and climbed over a wooden gate, then walked through new-growing grass towards a spot where she could see. A hundred yards away, at the foot of a steep slope, was a herd of Ayrshire cows, long horns hinting at fierceness, completely indifferent to her as they grazed.

Slowly, the bank came into view. The mass of yellow, waving gently in a slight breeze, was almost unbelievable; it was like a rippling field of gold. As she went on, picking her steps through wet grass and over muddy patches where the cows had trampled, she saw a small and shallow valley, a dell in which were oaks and birch and beech, mostly quite young, with that rippling fold stretching out in all directions. She had come upon a rare spot which was sheltered from bitter winds and which also trapped the sun, so that the daffodils here were in full bloom at least two weeks earlier than in most of the valleys and the open land.

The sun spread its warmth and brilliance over them; and bathed her, also. She stood transfixed. Shadows from small clouds darkened patches of the daffodils, thus making the rest of them seem brighter even than they were. The breeze not only made the heads of the flowers nod but rippled the surface of the tiny lake, the blue of which seemed edged with gold.

She had never known such peace.

She stayed where she was for twenty minutes, now walking, now resting, always going downhill, until she was on a level with the lake itself and looking across at the fields of gold, at eye-level. In a different way it was as beautiful as when she had first gazed down upon it. At last she turned away from the valley, but she could not stifle the desire to look back at the daffodils and when she was near the car take a last look at the reflection of the flower-clad bank in the lake.

Then she turned to her car, beyond the old five-barred gate.

It was gone.

She stared, startled, feeling almost stupid. She had no doubt where she had left it: at a spot some fifty yards away, in a natural clearing beneath several oak trees which gave ample room; any car, any ordinary vehicle, could pass on the narrow road.

So, why should anyone move hers?

She opened her bag quickly. Had she left the keys in the car?

No – they were here, on top of her leather purse.

Surely no one would *steal* her car from here! In a town, perhaps, or even near fast roads, but here – it made no sense at all.

At first she had been more astonished than alarmed, but gradually alarm and anger merged. She was miles from the main road, probably five or six miles from the nearest village, certainly just as far from the one she had come from. She had stayed the night at a farm on the outskirts of this village, enjoy-ing the smell of fresh baking, of bacon and eggs frying in a huge pan hanging from a hook over an open fire with a smell of smouldering peat. She had enjoyed the big double bed with its feather mattress and huge down quilt.

She wasn't thinking of that now, only of the car.

Who could possibly have taken it?

She studied the damp earth between the trees, seeing that several cars had passed this way and stopped here, but the prints of her car tyres were unmistakable. She could see where she had pulled off the road and where someone else had driven the car away.

Who? And *why?*

And – what could she do?

Obviously there was no point in staying here; a car might not pass for several hours. Well – even half an hour would be too long. She would have to walk on, and as she knew how far it was to the village from which she had come, she must walk towards it.

All her luggage was in the car.

Her jewellery. A reserve stock of money. Her clothes.

'Oh, it's damnable!' she exclaimed aloud.

She tried to remember but could not recall the sound of a car while she had been revelling in that idyllic view, but perhaps the steep fall of the meadow had cut her off from sound. At least she had on stout walking shoes, not the flimsy ones in which she always drove.

She strode on.

The sun was warm and the hills so green and beautiful, the ravines in the higher peaks still snow-filled although all the streams flowed past. Here and there was a waterfall only a few feet high, or else a series of miniature rapids, dancing and bubbling over stones and rocks smoothed by the years of running water made by melting snow.

The road ran downhill.

She rounded a corner, and saw an inn sign which made her heart leap! It was on a post stuck into the soil behind a stone-built wall; the black background and the white lettering were weathered and yet clean; the name was simple and so apt: *Dell View*.

There it was: slate roof sloping and showing beneath the leafless trees.

Suddenly her thoughts were distracted from her anger and bewilderment, for the inn overlooked the small lake and the valley of daffodils, hence, no doubt, its name. She did not pause to look at the view, only to glance as she walked on, for she was so anxious to get to the inn. It came into full view as she turned another corner, stone-built like the walls, the windows painted white, ivy growing over the front door which carried the name of the owner and the lawful legend: that he was licensed to sell alcoholic beverages and also cigarettes and tobacco.

Parked in sight was a green M.G. car, old-fashioned, with a stainless-steel luggage grid and canvas webbing straps and a hood folded down. She quickened her pace, then caught a glimpse of scarlet, the colour of her car.

There it was, safely parked, and vivid in the sun!

She could not know that the colour of her car was the same as the colour of her husband's blood after the bullet had struck him down.

Relief now softened the anger which Felicity Dawlish felt. She glanced at the windows, but no one appeared to be looking out. She took out her car keys and unlocked the boot. Her two cases were inside and did not seem to have been touched; certainly both where still locked. She looked into the interior of the car. There was her long coat, green and yellow and black tweed, flung carelessly over a raffia bag filled with fruit and soft drinks and a flask of coffee.

Pat had brought her that raffia bag when he had last been in Italy; he had promised her another, smaller, when he came back from this trip.

She smiled at the thought of him, and caught a swift mental picture of his face. She wondered what he would say had *his* car been stolen?

Stolen – or borrowed?

Was whoever had brought it here, still inside?

Her heart beat fast as she stepped to the door and opened it.

There was a tiny hallway with two doors leading off: *Public Bar* said one, *Saloon and Lounge* said the other. She opened the door of the public one. A fire blazed in an open grate and the flames reflected from the bottles on the bar behind the door. It was one of many small public houses which had one large bar, cut, as it were, into two, one half in the public and the other in the saloon bar. At slack times one barman could look after both. This one was empty, but a man out of sight sneezed.

She went into the room next door.

Except for a few round wooden tables, with chairs drawn up at each, this was identical with the other, although if anything the fire blazed higher and the air struck warmer. Standing at the bar was a young couple: a blonde girl in a mini and a dark-haired youth in what looked like a leather jerkin and corduroy trousers. Both glanced at her vaguely, a characteristic English attitude based on the assumption that one should not speak to a stranger unless the the stranger showed signs that he wanted to talk. The girl, pretty in a wide, soft-featured way, half smiled. The man's eyes lit up in admiration, and he stared intently before he looked away.

Felicity thought: Few Englishmen would be so bold; most would look away at once and steal their glances later.

A very tall woman, even taller than Felicity, who was five

feet ten, came from a door in the middle of the room and lifted the flap built in the bar. She was middle-aged, with iron-grey hair, and had a man's features, or at least masculine-looking lips and a square chin; but the expression in her eyes was gentle and compassionate.

'Good morning,' she said.

'Good morning,' replied Felicity.

They both fell silent; and the blonde and the man sat still and silent too.

'Can I help you?' asked the woman.

'I wonder if . . .?' began Felicity.

They fell silent again, but suddenly both laughed.

'I'm sorry,' Felicity said, 'but I've had a bit of a shock.'

'*Shock!*' echoed the blonde.

'I *am* sorry,' said the tall woman, as if with real concern.

The young man now watched with greater intensity, and had no reason to look away.

Felicity had an unmistakable feeling of tension She had known such feelings before when she had been with Pat, never when on her own. He had a nose for danger, and could sense when all was not well; it seemed to affect him like an electric current. Had he been standing next to her now, had he gripped her arm in the way he often did, just above the elbow, she would have felt as if he were passing on a warning.

That was the feeling she had now: of Pat, very close; of Pat, warning her.

But of what should she feel warned?

The tension was broken as the blonde picked up her glass, finished her drink, and slid off the stool. She squeezed the young man's hand and then went towards the door, over which was a sign: *Toilets*. As she vanished, Felicity asked the others:

'Did either of you see the red Morris Minor driven up?'

'Well, yes,' said the woman. 'A man got out and walked away. I thought he would come in for a drink, but it's nearly half an hour ago, and he hasn't turned up yet. Why, love?'

'It's mine,' Felicity said, helplessly. 'I parked it half a mile up the road, and someone drove it off.'

'What an astonishing thing to do!' exclaimed the woman.

'Is everything in it?' asked the young man. He had a faintly Cockney accent.

'Yes,' Felicity answered. 'Thank goodness.'

'Then it looks as if someone just wanted a lift,' suggested the young man dryly. 'Did you leave the key in the ignition?'

'No.'

'Lot of people do in London,' remarked the youth. 'Then they're surprised if their car gets pinched. Proper marvel, the way they can change the lock of a car overnight, repaint, new engine number, new tyres, new registration plates, the lot! Thousands of cars get nicked and are never found again. So you're lucky, lady!' He slid off his stool, said: 'Same again,' and went off to the door, leaving a newspaper on the bar.

'Can I get you something?' the bar-woman asked.

'*Could* I have some coffee?'

'Of course,' the other said. 'I'll go and get it – I was making some for myself.'

She lifted the flap again, and went out.

Felicity, still very puzzled and shaken because the sense of Pat being so near had been so vivid, moved along the bar and picked up the newspaper. It was folded to the sporting pages at the back – so like Pat! In fact, she supposed, like any man. She picked it up, unfolded, and turned over to the front page.

Pat's photograph was there: a huge one. Pat, smiling faintly; Pat, to the life!

And there was a screaming headline:

CRIME HATER DAWLISH – MURDERED
Shot on Rome's Famous Spanish Steps

Felicity stared down at that beloved face, not moving; hardly breathing.

The blonde opened the door very slowly and quietly and peered into the bar.

CHAPTER FOUR

THE REPORTS

FOR several minutes there was no sound.

The heaped coals, caked now from the burning, fell in the grate and flames leapt and hissed, but Felicity did not stir.

She thought in a curiously intent, desperate way: he can't be dead.

She swayed.

The blonde opened the door wider and stepped inside, but did not go far into the room.

Felicity felt a sudden onrush of emotion; not yet grief, this news was too sudden for grief, but of awful hurt. It was as if salt had been poured into her veins and was solidifying into one great mass of pain.

She said in a husky voice: 'Oh no, no.' And after a pause, she went on: 'Oh, please God, no.'

She was oblivious of the movements of the young couple, both of them now coming into the room as if oblivious of what had happened, although the blonde had seen so much. Firmer footsteps sounded, out of sight; the door opened wider and crockery rattled on a tray. The woman who had been behind the bar was massive, but fine-figured, handsome, imposing.

'Here we are,' she said, passing through the gap, 'And I've something very funny to tell you.'

Felicity heard her and yet did not really know what she said. The coffee was in a shining white porcelain pot, hot milk steamed in a matching jug. There were plain biscuits and some long fingers of rich-looking fruit cake.

'The man who brought your car down walked out into the woods, I'm told,' the woman said, setting out the cups. 'I'm going to have mine with you. You don't mind, do you?'

Then, for the first time, she noticed the change in Felicity; saw how still she was; how white; as if the blood had been drawn from her face.

'Oh, my goodness!' she exclaimed. 'What's the matter, love?'

The young couple drew nearer.

'What *is* it?' demanded the woman; and then she saw the open newspaper and Felicity's set stare.

'Oh, no,' she breathed. 'Oh, no.' There was a long pause, more tense than anything which had gone before; then she burst out: 'You're not his wife?'

Felicity swayed.

'What's the matter?' asked the dark-haired youth, moving closer. As Felicity swayed even more and began to shiver uncontrollably, he put an arm round her shoulders. The blonde gasped.

'It can't be. She ...' She glanced at Felicity, then at the photograph; gulped, and went on: 'They were asking for his wife on the radio.'

'I heard them,' the woman confirmed. She rounded the bar and took charge, putting one arm round Felicity's shoulders; compared with the man she was a giant. 'It's all right, love,' she went on with deep compassion. 'Come and sit down.' She guided Felicity to a wall seat near the fire.

Felicity began to recover a little from the shivering. The shock was still on her, and the pain, but she regained some measure of control. She knew that she must. Pull yourself together, she thought. The others became people instead of vague shapes and noises. The fire was warm on her legs, especially her left knee. The woman said to the girl: 'Bring the coffee, will you?' but it was the youth who fetched it.

'It *is* her,' he declared in an ejaculatory way. 'The wife. I saw a picture last night.'

'Oh, poor thing!' exclaimed the blonde, as if speaking of a cat.

'Drink some coffee,' the big woman urged. 'It will help you.'

'Brandy's what *she* needs,' said the youth, so worldly-wise.

'Must be an awful shock,' remarked the blonde. She looked and sounded as hard as the brass from which her hair took its colour. 'Can we do anything?'

'I know what I can do,' the dark-haired youth said. 'Phone

31

the newspaper. They said the police wanted to find her.' He moved off, looking about him, obviously for the telephone.

Felicity heard and understood all this.

She sensed the kindness of the big woman but had no sense of sympathy in the others. Sympathy? What did she want with sympathy? *Pull yourself together.* There was a cup of coffee in front of her, dark but not black; big fingers held a spoon and the coffee was being stirred vigorously. Felicity glanced up, forced a smile, and said: 'Thank you.' She sipped. 'I shall be all right. It was such – such a shock.'

'He is your . . . ?' The big woman broke off, as if hating the pain the word 'husband' would cause.

'Yes,' Felicity said. 'Yes.'

She sipped. The coffee was very hot and sweet, she didn't like the taste but knew that it was doing her good. Almost at once her body felt warmer; the ice melted. She sipped again. Her left side was very warm from the naked heat of the fire, and she shifted her position. Immediately the woman pushed a chair forward, making a screen.

Felicity said: 'I can't – can't believe . . .'

'There's no doubt about it,' stated the blonde. 'See what it says.'

The big woman's glance said: Be quiet, you little bitch. The blonde moved and picked up the newspaper which carried that huge photograph. In a moment of wild panic it seemed to Felicity as if she were picking up Pat's body, Pat's head. She drew in a sibilant hiss of breath. She could see the picture, which was so real and lifelike. *Pat – dead.* She drank more coffee.

'I'm all right,' she said, mechanically.

'Can I do anything?' The big woman was almost pleading. 'Telephone anybody?'

Felicity thought, Whom can I telephone? Her mother, up in Ayrshire, would know about this by now. If she, Felicity, had gone straight there instead of taking the day off she could have been with her mother when the news broke. She must get up to her quickly. How terrible her mother would feel. She – *she* loved Pat.

'Now don't hurry,' the big woman soothed. 'Don't hurry, love.'

'I must – I must get on.'

'You must stay here,' the big woman insisted. 'At least until you've seen a doctor. I'll telephone Dr. Willis. Don't worry, try not to worry.'

'But I must go to my mother. I . . .'

'Very soon,' the big woman soothed again. 'I'll tell you what, love – come into my sitting-room, it's more comfortable there. And don't *worry*,' she went on. 'You can't do anything, can you?'

Felicity cried: 'But I must!'

Her voice broke. She felt a flood of tears surge up within her, but they did not fall, seemed only to build up like a great wall behind her eyes. She allowed herself to be led away through the door and into a wide passage. The dark-haired youth was standing beneath a telephone hood; he stopped speaking as they passed. The woman pushed open the door of a room which had a glowing fire, television set, three large arm-chairs. A huge tabby cat sat on one of these. Felicity found herself being lowered into another chair. That wall of tears began to break; she closed her eyes and tears forced their way out and down her cheeks, in great, rolling drops.

'It can't be true,' she gasped. 'He can't be dead.'

'Pat,' she croaked.

'Oh, dear God, no, he can't be dead,' she sobbed. 'He can't be.'

The woman put the tray down on a table by the side of the chair, and poured out more coffee, then reached for a little bottle of brandy on a shelf by the fireplace and poured a little of it into the coffee. She saw the tears streaming down Felicity's parchment-white face. She did not try to make Felicity drink, after all, but went out and closed the door as the dark-haired youth spoke softly into the telephone:

'*No doubt at all. It hit her right between the eyes!*'

The woman of the inn did not hear his words.

A man sitting at a large desk on the first floor above a shop in London's Strand took that message from the youth in the Lake District. On one of the four walls was a large relief map of Europe; on one of the others was a similar one of the United States and Canada, with others of Mexico and South America alongside it. The third wall was a mixture: Australia, New Zealand and some Pacific Islands were close by Hong Kong and Singapore, India and Ceylon. According to these quite magnificently produced maps, the world came to an end at these countries; Russia and China did not exist.

The man himself was very broad-shouldered and, when sitting, looked extremely well dressed and groomed. His dark hair had a slight curl, almost a wave. His eyebrows and lashes were delicately formed; so were his features, with the exception of his very full, very red, moist-looking lips which gave the impression that his nose and chin were too small, so accentuating the size of his forehead. His white shirt cuff showed a gold cuff-link, his hands, shadowed with dark hairs, had well-shaped, manicured nails. He smiled as he held the earpiece, hearing the youth in the Lake District say clearly:

'*No doubt at all. It hit her right between the eyes.*'

The youth paused, what might have been footsteps sounded and the slamming of a door. 'The barmaid just passed, sir. I shouldn't hold on too long.'

'You have done very well,' the man in London approved. 'You shall be rewarded. Have you seen Clement?'

'He fixed the car, and then went off. There's a bus-stop about a mile away. I think he'll catch a bus.'

'Good,' the man approved, 'Excellent.'

'Will you tell the newspapers where she is?' asked the youth.

'I will see that they are told, Tony. Now you must ring off. I am expecting other calls.'

'Okay,' the man named Tony said. 'Good-bye.'

The man in the office said gently: 'Good-bye.'

He rang off, smiling as if with deep satisfaction. He stood up from his desk and stepped to the window, which was double-glazed and almost soundproof; only a faint murmur of street noises came through. Traffic moved at usual speed. Taxis and small cars whipped past the huge red buses, small vans were like wasps. He smiled more broadly, then burst into a chuckle, finally into a laugh.

A sudden build-up of traffic made a bus come to a halt immediately outside the window. In its window was a reflection, upside down, of the lettering above the shop window beneath him: *Celestia Travel*, it said, and in smaller lettering: *World Wide Travel Agents*.

A pretty girl looked at him from the top of the bus; obviously she thought he was trying to attract her attenion, and turned her head away. Almost at once she turned back and smiled, perhaps realizing that the distance between them spelt safety from wolves. He stopped laughing, but his face mirrored his delight.

The telephone rang, and he moved to it very quickly, gracefully for such a short man. Had he been tall, with such a breadth of shoulder, he would have been of a size with Patrick Dawlish.

'Signor Galli?' a girl said.

'Yes.'

'I have to tell you that the news was received at Scotland Yard with great alarm. They are horrified.'

'Are you sure?'

'I was told by an official in the Commissioner's office, a good friend of mine.'

'So! Good, good!' breathed Galli. 'You will pass on more information when you have it?'

'At once, Signor Galli.' The girl's soft voice faded, and he hardly heard her ring off. As he rang off in turn, he laughed again, and across that burst of cruel laughter the telephone rasped. He picked it up quickly; there was economy in all his actions, as if they were well-considered despite their speed.

'This is Signor Galli.'

'I can tell you, signor,' a man stated, 'That the news was received with consternation at the Home Office.'

'So!'

'The Under-Secretary himself was seen to turn pale, so important is this man.'

'That is excellent,' Galli said softly. 'It is very good indeed. Thank you.'

He rang off, rounded the desk, and sat down in a velvet-upholstered swivel chair. He turned the chair and leaned back, hands clasped, expression quite beatific. He closed his eyes, and was still and silent for what seemed a long time. He heard a sound at the door and looked up through his lashes. A woman in her thirties was in the doorway which was approached by a flight of carpeted stairs. She looked impressive in a long purple skirt and a white blouse. Her dark hair was drawn back from her forehead but groomed in a glossy half-halo which was held in position by two ruby or mock-ruby pins. She had dark eyes and an olive-coloured skin.

'Mario,' she said.

'Come in, Violetta.'

As she approached the desk, she smiled gravely and said: 'Jacob came into the shop.'

He started. 'Jacob!'

'Yes,' she said. 'He had been with some members of Dawlish's department, including Gordon Scott and some news-papermen. He says they were all appalled by the news. The newspapermen as well as the detectives.' She saw the way Mario's eyes blazed, and went on in a very quiet voice: 'Are the other reports in?'

'Yes. Yours is the last one,' Mario Galli told her. He clasped his hands together as he stood up, then spread his arms very wide apart. 'We can now be certain that Dawlish is dead!' She stood quite still, and he enfolded her in his arms and hugged her, then kissed her on either cheek. She permitted this, but did not respond. His face was radiant but her expression was quite sombre; his eyes glowed but hers were dull. 'Violetta!' he exclaimed. 'This is a great triumph, Dawlish is dead. It is a time for rejoicing!'

'It is time for sadness,' she declared.

'Nonsense! He was the one threat to our plans!'

'And for grief,' she insisted.

'Violetta, what is the matter with you? His death was a vital necessity.'

'Oh, yes. It was that, I know,'

'Then why this sadness?' Mario demanded.

'He was a great man,' she replied simply. On the desk was a newspaper with a photograph of Dawlish on the front page; it was the same photograph but not the same newspaper as the one Felicity had seen. Violetta turned it round so that they could both see it, and went on: 'He was a very great man.'

'He was a powerful enemy.'

'He was the only man who ever frightened you and the leaders of the Farenza,' she remarked.

'So, it is a triumph that he is dead!'

'And a tragedy,' she said simply.

Galli leaned away from her, studying her features and her expression closely, obviously unable to comprehend her attitude. Obviously she had affected him, dulling the edge of his delight and satisfaction. His forehead wrinkled and there was a deep furrow between his eyes. She did not look away from him, but a new expression crept into her face, making her cheeks very pale and taut. Or was it that Galli saw these things for the first time?

Suddenly, quietly, he said: 'What is it, Violetta? What was Dawlish to you?'

Very quietly she answered: 'I fought him bitterly for a long time. The more I saw of him and heard of him and studied him, the more I loved him. Do not ask me to rejoice, Mario. My love is dead, and I helped to kill him.'

CHAPTER FIVE

'MY LOVE IS DEAD'

VIOLETTA stood with Galli's arms about her, holding her lightly. She stared up at him without speaking again. He moved his right arm and placed his forefinger beneath her chin, tilting her head up and bending down, as if he were going to kiss her. He did not, but simply looked into her eyes.

'How long have you loved him?' he asked.

'Perhaps six months,' she answered.

'Did he know?'

'We seldom discussed any personal matters,' she replied. 'We were always very formal. I don't think he could possibly have guessed.'

'So he was not your lover.'

'He was not my lover.'

'Yet you loved him.'

37

'I came to love him dearly,' she said very quietly and with pride. 'Remember it was my task to study everything about him: what he did during the war, and after he was demobilized, how he fought crime so much by himself, and, of course, what he has done since he became officially a policeman. A picture emerged of a fine human being, Mario; a good man, a great man.'

'Violetta,' Mario Galli said. 'Why did you help to kill him?'

'It was part of my work.'

'How did you help?' he asked.

'All the information you have about him, and all the information about how much he learned about the Farenza, made you and the others decide that he must be killed. And I know it was inevitable,' she went on in a flat voice. 'I knew that whenever I was able to prove that he had taken one of our people prisoner, or was having others watched, that he was too dangerous to be allowed to live. I owe everything I have to the Farenza. I am part of it. I was in Italy, I have been for the five years I have lived in London. The Farenza's people are my people, the death of each one kills a little of me. I did not like what I had to do, Mario, but there was no way out.'

As she spoke, he could see the tip of her tongue against the back of her teeth, glistening momentarily as she formed some of the phrases. When she had finished he moved his forefinger from her chin and lowered his arms.

'I am sorry,' he said.

'It is over,' replied Violetta, in a flat voice. 'But do not ask me to rejoice.'

He shook his head. His full lips rubbed against each other and were very moist and it looked again as if he would bend his head a little further, and kiss her. He did not, but drew away.

His telephone bell rang, and he hesitated before turning away from Violetta and picking up the receiver. Suddenly his manner changed. He became, if not servile, then slightly over-polite.

'*Si*, signor,' he said. 'All of the reports are in, and they are all good ... *grazie*, signor! ... Yes, I will prepare the plans immediately ... Signor? If that is your wish, *si*, signor.'

After another moment he replaced the receiver, smiled at Violetta, and went on: 'The signor wished me to congratulate you.'

'Thank you,' Violetta said. But she did not smile, even in the knowledge of the approval of one of the leaders of the Farenza.

Felicity Dawlish had not smiled, except mechanically, since she had heard the news. Not all the understanding of her mother and the consoling efforts of friends helped her in any way. It was as if a great burden had been thrust upon her, so nearly intolerable that she did not know how long she could bear it.

Now she was in London: *their* home; with a man who represented Pat's chief – the Under-Secretary at the Home Office, a man obviously ill-at-ease.

'Mrs. Dawlish,' he said, 'The Home Secretary is extremely sorry that he cannot be here himself but he asks me to give you his deepest sympathy and commiseration, and also to say that he is sure some way will be found to make sure that your husband's services to the nation will be suitably acknowledged.'

Felicity thought: Sympathy and commiseration . . . suitably acknowledged. And she thought: My love is dead, how can they make up even for a hundredth part of him? She felt words welling up inside her: He can't be dead, he can't be dead! The small, dapper, very proper Permanent Under-Secretary concealed the alarm which suddenly attacked him, and extended his hand.

'If there is anything I can do, please don't hesitate – I repeat, *please* don't hesitate to call on me.'

'Thank you,' she said, quite formally.

He escorted her to the door. An older man, waiting, went with her along the broad passages to the lift and went down with her. At the door which overlooked Whitehall he bowed from the waist. When he straightened up she saw a new expression on his face, in his eyes. Until that moment he had been an automaton, but now the human being showed in the glow in his brown eyes, the colour in his cheeks, the slight quiver at his lips. But his voice was steady.

'I'm terribly sorry, Mrs. Dawlish. We – we, all of us – loved the major.'

Tears stung her eyes. 'Thank you,' she managed to say. 'Thank you.' She turned and walked off down the steps, into the broad thoroughfare. 'The major.' It was years since she had heard anyone call Pat 'the major' – his wartime rank. In those days everyone of lower rank and many high above had called him that. She turned into Whitehall. Traffic flowed, people walked, Big Ben towered above the great buildings across from Parliament Square. And Big Ben tolled its full range; it was eleven o'clock. Dah – dah – dah – dong! She heard this without noticing it until she reached the Cenotaph, so bare of decoration and with one small wreath of daffodils aslant on the lowest step. Dedicated to the millions who had died in two world wars! It was strange, it was ironic, to some it could be bitter, that there had been no new monument to the dead of the Second World War, she thought; this commemorates the fallen of the First World War, the fallen of the second were just tacked on to it. The Second World War. Pat's war. The major's war.

Big Ben finished the chimes and began to boom:

'One . . . two . . . three . . .'

In her mind the notes became a voice:

'Ma-jor! . . . Ma-jor! . . . Ma-jor! . . .'

Oh God, she couldn't stand it! Why had she been brought here at such a time? Two elderly women, passing, glanced at her in concern. A young man, coming across from Downing Street, stood and looked at her. She fought the tears back, and made herself walk more vigorously towards Parliament Square. Across the road, at the top of the old Scotland Yard building, was Dawlish's office.

It wasn't his any longer.

Another man came hurrying but did not simply stand and stare; he approached her. She didn't want to talk to anyone. But the young man fell in to step beside her, and was with her at the corner of Parliament Square and as she crossed it and passed the gates of the courtyard of the House of Commons. Two Members of Parliament, one of them familiar to millions on television and in the newspapers, glanced up and paused. Faintly, the voice of one reached her ears.

'Isn't that Dawlish's wife?'

At last she glanced at the man by her side. A young, strong-looking, fresh-complexioned man, she had come to know him well in the last few years. He was second-in-command so far as there was one to Pat in his work for the Crime Haters.

'Oh, Gordon,' she said in an agonized voice.

Chief Inspector Gordon Scott nodded. *Nodded*. He didn't speak, or even try to. His well-shaped lips were set tightly. His eyes were glistening much more shiny than she had ever seen them. He kept matching his steps with hers until they passed St. Stephen's entrance and the statue of Richard Coeur de Lion and, at an island, crossed the road. Only a hundred yards along Millbank and these old buildings was a group of modern office blocks of concrete and glass. At the top of one of these the Dawlishes had a penthouse flat. The wide, carriageway entrance was in a side street but within sight of the Embankment.

The doorman touched his cap as he hurried to press the call-button for the lift. The doors opened. Gorden Scott followed Felicity in and pressed the P.H. button. Now they had to stand face to face, but neither spoke. At the hall he stepped out firmly, but Felicity missed her footing. Don't let me cry, she prayed. Don't let me cry. She looked down, fumbling in her bag for the keys, took them out, dropped them. Instead of bending to get them she stood there with her head bowed. After what seemed an age later, Gordon's arm was about her shoulder, he guided her into the flat. There was a passage, doors leading off it, one door – open – leading to the huge room with french windows overlooking the magnificent panorama of the Thames as it flowed in its great loops past the new and the old, the history of London.

Felicity took off her hat and automatically poked her fingers through her hair – medium-coloured and clustered about her head. Gordon Scott said: 'I'll get a cup of tea,' and went like a dart to the kitchen, which led off here. In two of Dawlish's recent cases Gordon had spent some time here and so had learned his way about the flat. She thought, out of the blue, that Gordon had had his troubles – for him great ones – and this must be terrible for him, too. She put her hat on a small table by a huge armchair, one specially made for Pat because he was so large. She went to the window and looked over to St. Paul's and the Tower and Tower Bridge and the church spires and the modern buildings which appeared to be made of pile upon pile of children's bricks. She could *feel* Pat's arm about her shoulders, *hear* him say what he had said when they had first come here.

'This is our home, darling. Here and nowhere else.'

They had loved it; they had felt almost like royalty, high above all the rest of London, looking out of the window which stretched across most of the adjoining wall at Buckingham Palace and St. James's Park, Hyde Park and beyond.

'Fel – Felicity.' Only recently had Gordon begun to use her first name. 'Shouldn't there be someone here with you? A friend, a sister, someone …' He broke off. 'I don't mean to interfere but should you be here alone?' He had a cup of tea in his hand.

Felicity took the tea. 'I wanted to be,' she said.

'Yes, I daresay, but is it wise?'

'I don't know,' she admitted. 'I really don't know.'

'Wouldn't it – wouldn't it be better to go away for a while?' He was so distressed, his lips quivered as he spoke.

She sipped the hot tea.

'I would still have to come back,' she replied.

'Yes, but still … Are you … ?' He broke off.

'Am I going to Rome?'

'Yes.'

'I don't think so,' she said. 'The Commissioner asked me whether I would like to and I promised I'd tell him today.' She sipped again. 'If I don't go they will fly – fly him to London.'

Gordon Scott gulped.

'Er – yes. Where …? Oh, damn it, this is none of my business! I just hate to see you alone. I telephoned you this morning and they said you were out and no one was with you, and I knew you were going to see the Home Secretary, or his deputy, so I kept an eye open.'

'You're very kind,' Felicity said.

'*Kind*! If only I could – please!' He broke off. 'Please tell me to shut up, tell me to go to hell, and I will. But if I can help at all, I want to.' He was still showing difficulty in getting the words, he was so grief-stricken and yet embarrassed, so fearful of doing the wrong thing.

'Please stay,' she said. 'For a little while at least.'

'Of course!' He was delighted. 'Can I – is there anything I can do?'

'May I have another cup of tea?'

'Of course!' He almost snatched her cup, refilled it, and then began to talk more freely than he had before, on the move all the time. 'I wanted to fly straight to Rome but I had to stay in London, and – and take over. Childs is ill, he would have come back from his retirement but he's had the damned Mao flu and it's put him right out. *Someone* has to be in the office. I – oh, don't worry about this hour or two, there are plenty of bods to take over for a few hours, but ... Well, the truth is that nine out of ten of the reports that have come in since – since it happened – have been messages of sympathy. Shock. *Disbelief.*' He stood in front of her, his greeny-grey eyes with the irises golden brown glowing fiercely, and banged a clenched fist in the palm of the other hand. 'That's the awful thing. It doesn't seem possible. No one really believes it. Whenever I'm sitting in the office – I won't use his chair, I can't bring myself to – and the door opens. I look up expecting to see him.'

Felicity moved away so that he could not see her face; the way her lips puckered in anguish. The way her eyes were screwed up, fighting the tears.

She stared blindly out of the window.

Gordon Scott, obsessed by his own tragedy and involvement, went on in a taut, hurtful voice.

'And everyone who telephones says the same thing: "I can't believe it! I just can't believe it!" '

He spun round on her and saw her shoulders shaking; he stood absolutely still, his arms spread wide, his face a study in remorse. He muttered: 'What the hell's the matter with me? All I'm doing is making it worse.' He took a step towards her, hesitated, then heard a buzzing sound. Doorbell? He took another step, towards the door, heard the buzzing and realized it was the house telephone by the front door. He hurried towards it.

'Hallo.'

'Excuse me, sir,' said the doorman, 'but a lady is just coming

43

in – I'm nearly sure it's Mrs. Dawlish's mother. If it is, shall I send her right up?'

'Yes, at once,' Gordon said, in great relief. 'Yes, I'll meet her at the lift.' He put the receiver down and turned to Felicity, who was facing him now, much more composed. 'Apparently your mother . . .' he began.

Half an hour later he left them together. The last words he heard were from the tall, silvery-haired, broad-faced woman who had come so swiftly to her daughter.

'I can hardly believe it even now, darling. It just doesn't seem possible that it's true.'

'How is he?' the Italian surgeon asked.

'He is alive,' replied the German surgeon.

'Do you think he will live?'

'I think, now that he has a chance.'

'And – his mind?'

'First let us worry about his life,' the German surgeon retorted.

Soon afterwards when they left Dawlish in the ward where he had been taken after the first operation they were together in a small private room reserved for special visitors and V.I.P.s. Waiting for them was General Salvatorio, this afternoon dressed in a pearl-grey suit of immaculate cut; a polished-looking man, shorter than either the Italian or the German surgeon. He looked from one to the other, and waited.

'We are hopeful,' said the German surgeon.

'The Holy Mother be praised,' responded Salvatori. And he crossed himself. 'You understand the need for secrecy, gentlemen?'

'We have been suitably impressed,' answered the German, dryly.

'Nurses and assistants have been changed,' volunteered the Italian surgeon. 'The name of the patient on our records has been changed. I understand arrangements for the false identification of another man as Dawlish have been made.'

'That is so,' said Salvatori. 'Officially, Signor Dawlish is dead and his body has been taken from the hospital. This patient is now known as Mr. Danziger, a wealthy American who was involved in a road accident.'

'What you want is fully understood, and I shall say nothing,' the Italian surgeon said.

'And I shall also hold my peace,' promised the German. He had a very long, narrow face, and seldom smiled; but now he did, and his face lit up with a rare radiance, and his small mouth opened wide. 'To me, a patient is a patient, a brain is a brain. This patient's life will probably be saved. As I told my colleague we shall wait to see if he can also be saved as a normal human being. Will you answer me one thing, General?'

'If I can,' promised Salvatori.

'Why is it so important that the world should believe that this living man is dead? What can justify what is being done? Has he no wife? No children? No friends on whom great suffering is being inflicted? He must have some of these. So, why is this pretence being carried out? Answer me, please.'

Salvatori replied gravely: 'He is the one man whose death might make some extremely dangerous criminals careless. Although this man's wife and his friends and his relatives might suffer anguish, this pretence, as you call it, could save thousands, perhaps hundreds of thousands, of people from suffering even more.'

'How?' demanded the German, bluntly.

'I am sorry,' Salvatori said, 'but more I cannot tell you, yet.'

'I am not convinced that the proven suffering of one person can be justified by the possible saving of others,' retorted the German, 'but' – his smile was now very grave – 'the decision is not mine. I shall not betray your secret, but I shall expect an explanation when your effort has succeeded' – his voice dropped, his eyes took on a penetrating intensity – 'or failed.'

CHAPTER SIX

THE FARENZA

THE Farenza, as most of the world's police know, was in places as powerful as the Mafia – in fact in many places the two organizations were mistaken for each other, in other places they overlapped. There was no rivalry, as such; each accepted the existence and the rights of the other.

Like the Mafia, the Farenza was based on the family, or perhaps more truly on the tribe; one did not join, one was born into it. Like the Mafia it had its great families, virtually its aristocracy; and it had its small and comparatively poor ones. Some of those born into the Farenza lived on the fringe, some indeed had become absorbed in society beyond its borders, and these were seldom, if ever, called upon to work for the organization even in a trivial way. Many more had their daily jobs, in various strata of society. These were labourers and dock-workers, workers at the bench, skilled mechanics in the car and the aeroplane industries, in shipbuilding, construction work, in the manufacture of textiles, of synthetic fabrics, the makers of clothes, the growers and the processors of food.

There were many in local government services; in transport; in government offices. There were some in schools and many more in universities.

Most were called upon only to give information.

The Farenza was buried deep in the past of Italy, southern France, Spain and the Balkan states. It was widespread in the United States of America. It had its 'families' in all English-speaking nations, as well as in South America; and it was gaining a foothold in the newly emergent African states. It even had some 'families' in Russia, China and Japan, although these were used with extreme care.

The organization had a hard core of over five hundred full-time workers, and each of these was a specialist in some kind of crime. There were the killers, like the bearded man and the clean-shaven one who had shot at Dawlish and missed, later killed the girl, and escaped. There was the man who had been with the tourists and shot at Dawlish at short range – and escaped. There were bankers, lawyers, doctors and many in industry and commerce; there were the embezzlers, the informers, the saboteurs, the hold-up men, the bullion thieves, the jewellery thieves. There were members of the Farenza in every part of society. Information about big shipments of gold, for instance, or shipments of diamonds or of money, was passed on regularly. Companies which could be bought for a song and have their shares boosted artificially so that the new owners could make a killing were sought out and taken over.

There was in fact no kind of crime in which the Farenza was not active.

Some senior policemen had suspected this for a long time, although most had simply regarded it as a branch of the Mafia.

It had grown considerably since it had become so easy to cross frontiers; an aeroplane leaving New York with a valuable cargo could be hi-jacked in mid-air; ships could be taken over; every kind of daring crime was not only possible but practicable. Very careful plans had been made over the years to make it look as if each of these crimes was complete in itself: like that of the Great Train Robbery in England. In fact the success and the strength of the Farenza was based largely on ignorance of the police; on the assumption that the authorities would treat each crime as distinct in itself.

Dawlish had been one of the first policemen to believe that there was an organization responsible for many major crimes. Salvatori had also begun to suspect and Lohn, now in Brazil, was a third. A subcommittee of the Crime Haters had been set up to probe into the various activities and find the evidence which linked them. Once the Farenza had realized this, had discovered that Dawlish was the spearhead of the attack, they had set out to kill him. They knew that he had discovered a great deal and suspected more but as far as they could judge he had not yet made out reports. Nothing the other police leaders had done suggested that they knew anything like as much as Dawlish, and there was great reluctance to kill them also, and so inspire the greatest police search in this world's history.

The Farenza, of course, had its weaknesses: its greatest, perhaps, a sense of superiority, a kind of assumption of divine right. Especially among its leadership this had become inbred. It had for so long fooled or corrupted the police that it had never felt in danger from them as such. Even since there had been cause for alarm it had seen the danger as from Dawlish, not a loosely integrated police organization. And when the assurance of Dawlish's death reached the leaders throughout the world there was a great sense of relief; and overwhelming anxiety had been lifted – *Dawlish was dead, long live the Farenza!*

The Farenza, while it made its living out of crime and other means closely related to crime – the supplying of arms, for instance, to saboteurs or to revolutionary forces inside small countries – also had its benevolent side; it looked after its own. No one who worked even part-time for the Farenza ever went without food or the normal comforts of life, and wherever it was needed, work. It *was* like a huge, loosely knit tribal organization, and the part that showed was the benevolent one; it was also like an enormous Lodge, pledged to mutual help. Many of its families had no idea of how the money and the help received was earned.

For nothing was written down: everything about the organization was recorded in the minds of men. And some of those men were remarkable: such as Mario Galli.

So were some of the women: such as Violetta Casselli.

Violetta was a daughter of one of the ruling families, and from her infancy she had been trained to service and to loyalty. She knew more of the good than of the bad side of the organization, but since she had been selected to find out about Dawlish she had come into closer contact with the ugly aspect: the criminal side. Until this she had known the Farenza as a law unto itself: breaking the law of the land, as imposed on her and her family, did not matter: the real law which must always be obeyed was the law of the Farenza.

Now she was caught up in a conflict of loyalties.

For the first time in her life she had come to doubt the rightness of her own background; come to question the authority of the leaders of the Farenza, but her loyalty was firm.

It had not been really shaken as far as she knew, by what had happened to Dawlish: but as a woman she had been deeply hurt.

On the day when the two surgeons had talked to Salvatori, which was also the day when Felicity Dawlish's mother had arrived in London, she went home from the Celestia Travel Bureau, travelling by bus to Kensington High Street. She lived in a large, Victorian type of apartment building in a small flat on her own. Several Italian families lived in the building, and on the ground floor an Italian restaurant flourished, renowned among gourmets as having the best pasta in London. Nearby, in a row of small terraced houses, were other Italian families, with some Greek, French and Spanish, two White Russian and several other *émigrés* or refugees from behind the Iron Curtain.

The whole of this area was owned by a property company itself owned and controlled by the Farenza.

Violetta had to pass these small houses to get to her building, and outside one she saw more cars parked than usual, saw a front door open and grave-faced men going to and fro; this was in the house of one of the chefs of the restaurant. So she went to inquire.

'Benito and his friend Algoni are dead,' she was told. 'They met with an accident in Rome.'

She seemed to freeze as she realized the significance of what had happened: for Benito and Algoni had been the men who had attempted Dawlish's assassination, had failed but escaped capture. And she knew Benito. He was a cousin of a cousin, a member of her family by blood.

Benito, the bearded and plump assassin, and Algoni, the clean-shaven one, had been very pleased with themselves. Not knowing for certain what had happened they took full credit for Dawlish's death and for their own skill and courage in escaping. The Fiat had been parked and, when the police showed no outward sign of interest in it, driven to a garage in the southern outskirts of Rome, where its number and the engine number had been changed. They were trained killers; and they had learned to have eyes at the backs of their heads. This time they had felt quite secure from the police.

But, in fact, some of Salvatori's men had identified and were watching them, and other Farenza members learned this. With one of their men already in police hands, the Farenza dared not allow others to be caught. A police car was in sight of the little Fiat when, on the autostrada to Milan, an articulated lorry registered in Belgium had suddenly run out of control. The assassins had had scarcely time to feel fear; just one spasm as their hearts seemed to swell and then split asunder; then they had smashed into the huge truck which took the force of the impact almost with a shrug.

'The truck of the Euro-Economique Transport Co, is registered in Ghent,' the driver of the police car reported to Salvatori's chief agent.

'Treat the collision as an accident but have the truck followed and ask Belgium to investigate the company,' the chief agent ordered. He was a tall man for an Italian, with round shoulders and too corpulent. He made a note and then looked up at Neil Commyns, who was in the office with him.

'So the Farenza has shut two more mouths,' Commyns said laconically.

'Undoubtedly,' agreed the agent. 'And that is surely evidence of their alarm, which is good. Also' – he smiled with obvious satisfaction – 'they have I think opened another source of investigation.'

'The Euro-Economique Transport Company,' Commyns hazarded. 'I seem to have heard of that before.'

'We shall probably hear much more,' remarked Salvatori's agent. He stood up from his desk in a small office in a building opposite as Salvatori himself came in. He saluted. 'Good afternoon, General. I have just heard . . .' He repeated what had happened and Salvatori nodded in approval of everything he had done.

Almost immediately, Salvatori and Commyns went out of the office and into Salvatori's own. This was four times as large, very plain, and shadowed because of the wooden shutters being closed. Salvatori motioned to a chair and dropped into his own, which seemed a little too large for him; so did the flat-topped desk with a small battery of telephones and neatly arranged files.

'Neil,' he said, 'it is very obvious that Dawlish was right. The Farenza has branches in several other countries. Did you get the report from Gordon Scott about what happened in the North of England?'

'Yes,' replied Commyns, stretching out his long legs. 'Apparently Mrs. Dawlish was watched and followed, and her reaction to the news was observed. And there are indications that the reactions of politicians, as well as some of Scotland Yard senior officials, were also checked.'

'Yes,' Salvatori said.

'How has Mrs. Dawlish taken it?' demanded Commyns.

'She is grief-stricken.'

'I'm still not sure we've done the right thing,' declared Commyns. 'I'm a long way from sure.'

'I am more than ever sure that we had no alternative,' declared Salvatori, spreading his hands over the desk. 'The Farenza is now convinced that he is dead. They were obviously very much afraid of him. They may now become increasingly bold, and we may soon learn much that we need to know.'

'The "accidental" death of the two men doesn't suggest that anyone is being careless,' Commyns objected. He linked his fingers over his flat stomach. 'How much do we know of what Dawlish knew?'

'A great deal now,' answered Salvatori, taking out some keys. 'Enough for us to act with caution and get the results he most wanted. He allowed himself to be attacked or made himself vulnerable so that we could catch the assassins and act more quickly, but . . .' He unlocked a drawer in the side of his desk and groped with his fingers, without looking. 'Patrick sat in this very office a few days ago and recorded what he had discovered. He wanted to tell me but I was called away by the Ministry, so I had to leave him alone. However, the tape recorder is here with the tape in it. I was present when he wound it back and then checked that his voice had been properly recorded.'

Salvatori stopped speaking.

His expression changed and alarm touched his eyes. He looked down, and stayed just where he was. His lips moved, but Commyns did not hear what he said. Commyns himself stood up and leaned across the desk. Salvatori's right hand was touching the side of the drawer, which had some files in it but no tape recorder that Commyns could see.

Salvatori said in a harsh voice: 'It has gone.' He looked up. 'I placed the tape here only an hour before leaving with Dawlish for the Spanish Steps. It has been – it could only have been stolen.'

Commyns asked sharply: 'Can you trust your staff?'

After a long pause the Italian answered: 'I thought I could. Three have access . . .' He broke off. 'I shall not discuss it here,' he went on in a low-pitched voice. 'But I will set some traps. Meanwhile . . .' He took out a pale blue silk handkerchief and wiped his forehead. 'Meanwhile I will not tell anyone else that I have discovered the loss.'

He closed and locked the door, and straightened up. His eyes looked huge and over-bright, his lips were set in a thin line. Commyns now moved to his chair but did not sit down. It was a long time before he asked:

'Did Dawlish leave any record in England?'

'He told me this was the first note he had made of the Farenza investigation.'

'And he didn't tell you more?'

'Only that he expected another attack – and we learned that it would come on the Spanish Steps. It was obviously believed that with so many people about the assassins could get lost in the crowd, and escape.'

'So, no one has any idea what Dawlish knows,' Commyns said, ignoring the last remarks. 'It couldn't be much worse.'

'It could not be any worse,' Salvatori declared. He wiped his forehead again and looked oddly at Commyns, hesitating as if he did not quite know how to say what he needed to say. He glanced at the door where a secretary was sitting. He turned and looked out of the window. At last he stood up, and Commyns could not fail to see how bloodshot his eyes were, how pale his face. 'There is just one person to whom he might have spoken.'

Commyns asked: 'Who? His assistant in London?'

'No,' replied Salvatori. 'No. Oh, that is possible but unlikely. Dawlish made some discoveries which he liked to turn over in his mind. He did not like to think aloud, he would often joke that he did not want others to think how badly he put his thoughts together. But he did sometimes think aloud to one person.'

Commyns caught his breath and formed two words: 'Oh, no.'

'He sometimes talked aloud to his wife,' Salvatori went on, as if he had no doubt at all.

CHAPTER SEVEN

SPECIAL MISSION

COMMYNS did not speak, but placed his hands at the back of his neck and looked at the Italian. It was very quiet and still in the office. Salvatori turned back to the desk as if he meant to open the drawer again; instead, he moved some papers and rummaged through other drawers.

Commyns said 'Luigi, do you know what you've just said?'

'Yes,' answered Salvatori. 'I know exactly.'

'You can't send a man to ask Dawlish's wife if she can recall anything her husband said about this.'

'Why not,' asked Salvatori.

'It isn't human.'

'Neil,' said Salvatori, 'You are too soft-hearted.'

'I don't think you get help out of anyone by playing on their grief.'

'You can by playing on their anger,' Salvatori retorted.

'Or their hurt.' Commyns began to move his hands, still linked behind his neck, his elbows jutting out as if he were wearing swimming-pool wings. 'Are you suggesting that we try to persuade Mrs. Dawlish to help so as to enable her to avenge her husband?'

'Vengeance can be a powerful weapon,' Salvatori declared, simply.

'No!' exclaimed Commyns, bringing his arms down sharply.

'I didn't agree about pretending he was dead. It would have been much better to tell the truth: that he's at death's door. The effect in the short term would be the same, and we wouldn't have all this lying and conniving to do. I don't like it at all, and I strongly oppose asking Mrs. Dawlish to help . . .' He broke off for a moment and a new expression entered his eyes. 'Unless you tell her the truth,' he added less sharply. 'I would go along with that. I wouldn't feel that we were tormenting her if she knew there was some hope.'

When Salvatori stood without answering, Commyns went on in a sharper voice: 'She'll have to know that it's an outsize lie before long. Presumably,' he went on, his voice oozing sarcasm, 'you are not going to deny the widow a last look at her dead husband's face.'

Salvatori said: 'I did not know you were so soft-hearted.'

'I think I see facts,' Commyns said. 'And . . .' He broke off, with a half-frown. 'Oh, forget it.'

'Please,' Salvatori urged. 'What were you going to say?'

'It doesn't matter.'

'It may matter a great deal.'

Commyns moved again, restlessly, and yet with complete contrast. He was nearly as tall as Dawlish and quite broad, but much more rangy and less solid, and far less massive. His weathered face with the sun-carved lines made him look older than Dawlish. In its way that face was extremely impressive.

'Luigi,' he said, 'you're an Italian.'

'So?'

'And Pierre-Jacques is a Frenchman.'

'So?'

'And Lohn is a Brazilian.'

Salvatori said slowly: 'Yes. Yes,' he repeated, 'I think I begin to see. You are an Anglo-Saxon. So was Dawlish. So is Mrs. Dawlish. And . . .' He smiled with humour for the first time since he had discovered that the tape-recording was missing: 'Anglo-Saxons understand Anglo-Saxons better than any southern Europeans or South Americans do.'

Commyns' expressions relaxed.

'Yes,' he agreed. 'That's exactly what I mean.'

'And you think Mrs. Dawlish would be more likely to be able to help if she knew that her husband was alive, because anything she recalls might keep him alive. Whereas, you reason, a Latin wife might be more moved by vengeance than rescue.'

Commyns actually chuckled. 'Subconsciously,' he declared. 'All of these reactions would be subconscious.'

Salvatori nodded, very slowly and deliberately.

'The Anglo-Saxons are a remarkable people,' he observed at last. 'Carlos Lohn will be back tonight. We shall all four dine together in private, and then we shall be able to decide what to do. Three Latins and one Anglo-Saxon. Do you think the odds are fair?' Laughter began to sparkle in his eyes.

Commyns pondered for a moment and then said with pursed lips: 'I don't know, but I'm sure Dawlish would think they were.'

After a moment of startled silence Salvatori threw back his head and laughed aloud; it was the first time for days that he had laughed or even felt as if he could.

'One thing has not been realized,' Pierre-Jacques said.

'What is that?' asked Salvatori.

'Only one?' asked Commyns, dryly.

Lohn, who had arrived in Rome after the crisis in Brazil only two hours ago, looked glassy-eyed, as if he needed a lot of sleep to make up for what he had lost in two long flights across the Atlantic, made no comment. He was, as always, immaculate and reserved to a point of aloofness.

'If Mrs. Dawlish sees and identifies the body the last possible doubt in the minds of the Farenza will be gone,' Pierre-Jacques said. When the others waited for him to go on he added: 'In order to identify it, she must be told in advance what to do.'

'So someone will have to tell her that we lied to her,' remarked Commyns.

'You are too literal,' Lohn put in unexpectedly. 'A mistake was made by the surgeon, by the doctors. It was believed he was dead. By a miracle of surgery and treatment he was revived. Is that not simple?'

Salvatori was smiling; Pierre-Jacques pursed his lips and nodded.

'It must certainly be handled with great delicacy,' he declared. 'I do not know Mrs. Dawlish well, but I have every reason to believe that if it is possible for her to help, she will. Neil – will you fly to London and talk to her?'

Commyns protested: 'But I don't know her at all!'

'I think perhaps that is an advantage,' replied Pierre-Jacques. 'She is utterly charming and most forbearing, but she is very, very English in attitudes and outlook. I think she will always have a slight if subconscious suspicion of all Latins. Don't you, Luigi?'

He looked startled when, for the second time that day, Salvatori burst out into laughter. Commyns chuckled, while Lohn looked from one to the other as if he could not understand this levity in such circumstances.

'It is too difficult to explain,' Salvatori said, 'but we were discussing the differences between Anglo-Saxons and Latins only this afternoon.' Pierre-Jacques and Lohn raised their hands in acceptance of that explanation, and the Italian went on: 'Neil, you will go to see Felicity Dawlish, won't you?'

Commyns considered for what seemed a long time before he replied: 'Yes, I will.'

Felicity was in the kitchen of the flat so high above London when the telephone rang. Her mother was unpacking in the spare bedroom, for they had talked and cried and talked again for hours. Felicity felt as if all the strength had been drained out of her, everything she did now was with an effort. Every now and again her mind seemed to go blank, and she would recover herself to find herself standing with a cup in her hand, or something from the larder, without remembering why she had wanted it. The telephone broke across a mood soon after she had set her teeth and determined *I must pull myself together*. She moved to the white telephone near the kitchen door, where several oddments stood by the instrument on the working surface.

She picked the receiver up.

'This is Mrs. Dawlish.'

'There is a call for Mrs. Felicity Dawlish from Rome,' said the operator.

Felicity caught her breath as if in sudden pain, and to gain a moment's respite she asked: 'From where?' Rome, Rome, Rome; Pat, oh my darling Pat.

'From Rome, Italy,' the operator repeated.

'This – this is Felicity Dawlish,' Felicity's voice was very husky.

'Hold on, please,' said the operator.

Felicity drew up a stool, and sat down; her legs wouldn't support her any longer. Rome. Until the day before yesterday she would have been sure this was Pat. Oh, dear God, Pat! Tears stung again and she hated herself for her weakness and yet could not keep them back. Her hand was aquiver, the receiver rattled against the handle of a milk jug. *Rome.*

A man spoke in good English but with a marked accent and American overtones. 'Am I speaking to Mrs. Felicity Dawlish?'

'Yes,' Felicity managed to say. 'Yes.'

'This is Luigi Salvatori,' the man announced. 'First, I am very sorry, very sorry at what has happened. It is not possible to find words.'

'Please – please don't try,' Felicity said. Salvatori, a friend of Pat, a man she had often met. Would he call just to say how sorry he was?

'I wish that I could come myself to see you,' said Salvatori, 'but my other duties prevent that for the moment. To represent all of us who are in the conference, however, we have asked Captain Neil Commyns of the Chicago police to come and see you.'

'There is no need . . .' Felicity began.

'He will be with you by eleven o'clock tonight,' interrupted Salvatori, 'and he will bring with him the good wishes and understanding of us all.'

Felicity muttered: 'Thank you, thank you.' But this man Commyns was a stranger, why should so many old friends send a stranger?

'If there is anything at all . . .' began Salvatori.

Oh, what a fool, Felicity thought helplessly, what an utter fool. Who could do anything? He meant so well, this Neil Commyns would mean so well, but what could anybody do or even say? Why didn't they leave her alone? That was unreasonable, she *was* unreasonable, she did not know what to do. She said something without fully realizing what it was, and replaced the receiver. Immediately, she hoped she hadn't been rude. Salvatori was a nice man, good and clever, and Pat liked – *had liked* – him a lot. She had only met him at social occasions connected with the Crime Haters, and she didn't know Neil Commyns at all. Pat had talked about him once or twice lately, and had been non-committal. That was partly because he had replaced Randy Patton who had been a delegate to the Crime Haters for years. He had told her there was some kind of rivalry between New York and Chicago.

Goodness!

He was due here at eleven o'clock and it was already half past nine. She must tidy up, dress, get a meal for herself and her mother – she hadn't a moment to spare.

The next hour was the first, since the news of Pat, when she hadn't been obsessed by thought of and grief for him. She *had* to look the best she could, had to make up a little, had to, had to, had to . . .

Her mother came, and listened.

'I'll get something ready to eat,' she promised. 'You just worry about yourself.'

At five past eleven the front-door bell of the flat rang. Felicity in a dark green dress trimmed with brown, both simple and elegant, opened the door to find Gordon Scott and a stranger who stood nearly a head taller than Scott. He had a curiously carved-looking face and eyes which caught the light from the hall and seemed to spark.

'I haven't come to stay,' Gordon said, 'but I met Captain Commyns at the airport and brought him here, to . . .'

'Vouch for me,' Commyns put in, dryly. 'How are you, Mrs. Dawlish?'

His gaze was steady, his grip firm but unlingering. He had rather long, thin lips which puckered at the corners. She liked him at first sight. Scott would not come in beyond the passage but made off, and Felicity led Commyns into the big room. Her mother had gone to bed and would read until she was sure there was no need for her. Commyns took one appraising look about the room, and at once she led him towards the corner windows. The dial of Big Ben was still alight and the tower floodlit; St. Paul's and most of the other buildings, old and new, were also floodlit, and all the more impressive because it was a moonless, starlit night. She stood by him for a few moments, calmer than she had expected to be. She sensed that this stranger had some quality in common with Pat: a rock-hardness whenever it was necessary. When he turned to look at her his eyes were in shadow but the spark was still in them.

'Mrs. Dawlish,' he said. 'I think the formal way to say what I have to say is: please be prepared for a shock.'

A *shock*, she thought, astonished. Another shock?

She had a strange feeling, that although his lips hardly moved, he was smiling.

'Shock,' she said aloud. 'Haven't I had shock enough?'

He didn't reply at once, and she didn't go on. She felt a stab that was almost pain, followed by a fierce surge of hope which showed unmistakably in her eyes. She raised her hands in front of her breast, and her lips parted slightly.

'I think you are already half-prepared,' he went on. 'We are not yet sure how fully he will recover, but your husband is not dead.'

She gulped, echoed the two words, felt as she had when she had first seen the newspaper in the saloon bar of the inn. Suddenly her knees went weak, and as suddenly this man had an arm about her waist and was leading her to a chair away from the window, and helping her to sit down. She leaned her head against the back of the chair, and after a moment she asked in a barely audible voice:

'You *are* sure?'

'Yes,' he said. 'He was – thought to be dead.' She wondered at the hesitancy but it didn't matter; for now it didn't matter. Her heart was beginning to thump. 'But there was a response to a late stimulation by drug and electrolysis. He will live. There is anxiety about what his mental condition will be when he comes round, but a great deal of hope. Just before I left Rome I studied the latest reports from the surgeons. I have copies with me.'

'Pat,' she sighed. 'Pat.' Then in a sharper voice: 'Have you seen him?'

'No one has, except the medical team,' Commyns answered.

He pulled up another armchair and sat on the arm. 'Will you have something to drink? A brandy, perhaps?'

'Yes,' she said, making to get up. 'And you . . .'

'Tell me where to find the brandy.'

'I would rather get it myself.' Felicity stood up and walked to a corner cabinet, pulled down a shelf and revealed bottles and glasses. She did everything quickly, nervously, and talked all the time. Not dead, not dead, not dead was like a mighty chorus in her mind and heart. 'I shall be all right. I've often thought him dead, but this time – this time I think I believed it. What do you mean by "his mental condition"? You don't mean that he might never really recover the use of his senses, do you? I don't know which would be better for him, to be dead or only half-alive. *Is* that what you mean?'

'The report will tell you that he is not now believed to have serious brain damage, but for a long time he may have to live at half-pressure.'

She handed Commyns a large brandy glass, and picked up a smaller one for herself.

'He will hate that,' she said. *He was alive, alive, alive!*

'Won't he consider himself lucky to be alive at all?' asked Commyns.

'I don't know. Obviously no one can tell until . . .' Felicity broke off, and added: 'Don't take too much notice of me – he's alive! Oh, thank God!' She fought and regained her self-control. 'I couldn't believe he was dead at first, now I can hardly believe he's alive!' After a moment she went on: 'Are they *sure* there's no major brain damage?'

'They feared there was. They now say no.'

'Thank God!' breathed Felicity. She sipped her brandy and then crossed to the window, looked out in silence for some time and then over her shoulder at Commyns. 'When can I see him?' she asked. *He's alive.*

'If you will do what I and the others of the governing committee of the conference want, not for some time,' Commyns said, and when she tautened up and turned towards him, as if aggressively, he went on: 'He was fighting an organization called the Farenza. They think they have killed him. We want them to go on thinking so, at least until he is well enough to help us track his assailants down, and so keep him out of danger.' When she stared with a mixture of doubt and defiance he went on: 'We want you falsely to identify another man's body as your husband's, Mrs. Dawlish. And we want you to tell everything, absolutely everything, he has said to you about the Farenza, or a new case of importance; anything which may conceivably have a bearing on the case he was investigating. We need your help because for the time being we can't have his.'

CHAPTER EIGHT

FALSE WITNESS

THE moment he set eyes on Felicity, Commyns thought: God, she's a handsome woman. And he thought: Yes, handsome, not exactly beautiful; she moves and stands like a queen. Throughout that first tense period of meeting he had chosen his words with great care and judged her reaction with equal care. When at last he told her what he wanted her to do he had no doubt at all that she would agree. He wondered what was going on in her mind; if he judged rightly, the white-hot grief had passed before he had arrived and she had almost adjusted to her husband's 'death'. Now there was urgent need for re-adjustment.

'I don't know what I can do to help,' she said.

'Until now you hadn't known there was any need,' Commyns countered. When he smiled at her freely his face had a slightly droll expression, and the lines at his eyes and the mouth became much deeper. 'Would you like to sleep on this and decide what's best to do in the morning?'

'No,' she answered, 'I would rather think and talk about it now.' She pursed her lips. 'There's one other person who has to know the truth.'

'Who?' demanded Commyns.

'My mother. She is staying here, and it would be odd to ask

her to leave, impossible for her to be here without telling her about Pat. I couldn't deceive her convincingly.'

'Surely, you must tell her,' agreed Commyns.

'I think I will at once,' decided Felicity. 'Will you excuse me while I go to her?'

'Of course,' said Commyns. 'May I use your telephone meanwhile?'

'Please do,' Felicity said.

He thought: She has remarkable self-control; she is a remarkable woman, as he watched her go into the passage. A door opened, she said something to her mother, and the door closed. Commyns went immediately to the telephone and dialled Dawlish's office number. Gordon Scott answered instantly.

'Deputy A.C.'s office.'

'This is Captain Commyns,' Commyns announced.

'I hoped it was,' said Scott. 'How is Mrs. Dawlish, sir?'

'Rather better than I'd hoped,' replied Commyns.

Scott said huskily: 'Good.'

'Were we followed?' asked Commyns.

'No.'

'Is there any evidence that I was followed from Rome?'

'No,' Scott repeated. 'None at all.'

'Is this building watched by the Farenza?'

'We think it was until early this morning, but there have been no strangers watching it since,' replied Scott.

There was a pause before Commyns said rather heavily: 'The body should be in London by ten o'clock tomorrow, and arrangements for cremation will have to be made.'

'They have been,' said Scott, in a brittle voice. 'At Golders Green crematorium. There will be a service at the crematorium chapel at twelve noon. Mrs. Dawlish said earlier today that she would prefer the – prefer her husband to be taken straight to Golders Green, and she herself will be there at half past eleven.'

'I shall escort her if there is no close relative,' Commyns said. 'Will you be there?'

'Yes,' Scott said, 'so will half the senior officers at Scotland Yard, as well as the Commissioner, Assistant Commissioners and Commanders. It – it is going to be a very impressive funeral, Captain.'

'I imagine so,' Commyns said. 'Yes. Thank you.'

'Glad to do everything I can,' Scott replied. 'Good night.'

'Good night.' Commyns rang off, but almost immediately put through a personal call to Salvatori at his apartment overlooking the Tiber on one of the seven hills of Rome. From where Commyns sat he could see the great dome of St. Paul's, silvered by the spotlights; and he could see the tops of lesser buildings, too. Very soon the call came through and Salvatori said at once:

'How is Mrs. Dawlish?'

'Holding up very well,' Commyns replied. 'I was able to help a little.'

'I am very glad,' said Salvatori. 'What is the situation in London?'

'There appears to be no suspicion,' answered Commyns. 'But is this really . . .?'

'It is quite safe,' Salvatori interrupted.

'I'm very glad to hear it,' replied Commyns sardonically. 'Before the funeral . . .'

'Yes?'

'Did you expect a kind of cortège?'

'Cortège?' Salvatori groped for the word's meaning.

'The Commissioner of Police, all the seniors, some ministerial officials . . .'

'But of course, *la corteggio*,' Salvatori interrupted quickly. 'How else could it be made convincing?'

'What will these officials say when the truth is known?'

Salvatori was silent for a long time, and a slight buzzing and squeaking on the line became more noticeable. Afar off, there was the sound, more like an echo, of voices. An aeroplane sounded, red and green lights showing like stars from another galaxy. There was a rustle of papers, Commyns shifted his position, sitting upright and frowning, as if the waiting puzzled and displeased him. At last he was driven to ask:

'Are you there?'

'*Si*,' replied Salvatori. '*Si*. One moment more, please.'

Much more than 'a moment' passed; a minute, at least, with papers still rustling. Then Salvatori said:

'Neil.'

'Yes?'

'On twenty-seven occasions, according to my notes, you have raised an objection to what we are doing. Twenty-seven,' the Italian repeated. 'We agreed earlier tonight, all four of us, and yet you object again. Why are you so adamant?'

Slowly, Commyns replied: 'Because I'm not convinced that it's right, I guess. Once he is officially buried, then the day must come when the whole world is going to know it was fooled. That means that all the world's police forces, governments and newspapers will know.' He paused for a moment and then went on: 'I don't think they are going to like it.'

'They will dislike the continued success of the Farenza much more,' declared Salvatori.

'I wonder how right you are,' remarked Commyns.

'Captain,' Salvatori said stiffly, 'if you prefer not to continue with your part in these tactics I am sure one of us will replace you. But please remember it was a unanimous decision and since none of the action planned is in the country you represent, you are bound by the decision at least to silence.'

After a pause Commyns said: 'I suppose so. I don't know that I want to withdraw, Luigi. I want to be sure nothing is overlooked.'

'Is that all?' Salvatori sounded stiff and unbending.

Commyns chuckled, and his expression changed, as if he derived some deep enjoyment of the situation.

'I am not a Farenza agent, if that's in your mind!'

'Such an obdurate manner could not be expected from such an agent,' Salvatori said, still unbending. 'If you were you would be glad to pretend to do everything we wanted. I don't doubt your integrity. I am beginning to doubt whether you will be able to do your best, since you have so little enthusiasm.'

'I guess you're right,' conceded Commyns. 'After high noon tomorrow all our boats will be burned, and we won't be able to change our minds then. I'll stop putting up the arguments.'

'I do not think there will be any need to change our minds,' said Salvatori. 'Tell me one thing: is Mrs. Dawlish reluctant to help? Is that a factor in your attitude?'

Commyns caught a movement out of the corner of his eyes. He shifted round, the better to see Felicity coming into the room. She was freshly made up, moved with the now familiar gracefulness, and looked at him gravely.

'Not in the slightest,' he answered Salvatori, 'I just want to be sure we don't regret anything we're doing. Good night, Luigi.' He replaced the receiver and stood up, smiling more freely. 'I wish I knew these men as well as your husband does,' he said to Felicity. 'They are sure this is the right thing to do.'

'Aren't you?' asked Felicity sharply.

'I do have some doubts,' Commyns admitted. 'I wonder what your police commissioner will say when he eventually hears the truth.'

'He will say what Pat would say,' Felicity answered promptly.

'And what would that be?'

'It has been justified if it succeeds,' said Felicity. 'And was bad policy if it doesn't help to catch the Farenza.'

'My,' breathed Commyns. 'I see.' He picked up his brandy glass which was nearly empty, and went on, putting his thoughts into words: 'You speak very easily of the Farenza.'

'It is a very familiar word to me,' said Felicity.

He looked surprised. 'Did your husband talk about it often?'

'He seldom talked about it,' she answered. 'He often mentioned it.' She gave a little laugh. 'At one time if anything happened which we didn't understand he would lower his voice to a sepulchral tone, and say. *"It must be the Mafia"*. For the past few months he changed to: *"It's the Farenza"*, in the same tone.' She laughed, a natural enough sound. 'Are you married, Mr. Commyns?'

'Divorced,' he said. 'So I'm in my second bachelorhood.' His eyes matched hers in the laughter. 'After ten years of constant conflict.'

'Then you might not understand,' Felicity remarked.

'Understand what?'

'The relationship between me and Pat,' she told him. 'We have been married a long time. Even during the war I never knew whether he would come back from a mission – no more than I do now. We could never talk much about the danger, and he never believed in letting me know too much about any particular case, believing that if I knew much then I might be in danger, too.'

'That's the way I think,' interpolated Commyns.

'Well,' she said. 'We couldn't talk seriously about it, we didn't want to pretend the situation didn't exist, so we made a kind of joke. If we had a near miss in the car, he'd often say, "It's the Mafia", or "It's the Farenza", or "Someone thinks I'm James Bond." Somehow it eased the tension.'

She looked at Commyns as if wanting to ask: Do you see what I mean?

He said: 'I don't really know Pat well, Mrs. Dawlish. I'm beginning to want to very much.'

Quietly, she responded: 'Thank you.' And then her eyes glowed. 'If he were here, you would be Neil, I would be Felicity. What *is* really worrying you, Neil?'

'Can you put on the act?' asked Commyns, flatly.

'Yes,' Felicity answered, as positively.

'And should we?' asked Commyns.

'That's up to you and the others,' she replied. 'I think Pat would say "yes". We didn't talk seriously about the Farenza but I do know he was very worried about it. Once or twice, when something had gone wrong, he would say: *"It's worse than the Mafia."* And sometimes he would turn very broody and contemplative, the way he always did when things weren't going right. One thing I can tell you for certain.'

'What's that?' Commyns asked.

'He was *really* worried about the Farenza.'

'Have you any idea why?' asked Commyns. He spoke casually, but there was fresh spark in his eyes and there seemed new tension in him. 'Any idea at all, Felicity?'

She didn't answer at first.

Commyns had a strong feeling that she knew her husband extremely well, was in tune with his moods, shared most of his anxieties if not all of his problems. He recalled a story of the help she had given Randy Patton when at a Crime Haters conference in London; Randy had been in deep trouble with his wife.* Now he was sure that she was searching her mind before answering his question.

Then she said: 'Yes and no.'

'That doesn't really help much,' Commyns retorted.

*A Clutch of Coppers

'I can only tell you the truth,' Felicity pointed out. 'He was convinced but had no proof that the Farenza was planning a very big coup. I think he thought it could be on an unprecedented scale. Almost – deadly.'

He waited, but when she didn't go on asked quietly:

'Deadly in what way?'

'I can't be sure,' Felicity answered. 'But I think he thought they were getting too big for their boots, and believed themselves strong enough to defy the police everywhere. And that would be a challenge to national security.'

'*This* nation's?'

'He isn't a little Englander,' she answered. 'He's as English as can be in spite of the name Patrick, but he thinks in global terms.' She spoke intently now, and seemed to be looking for some guidance; looking as a seer might look into a crystal ball, trying to pierce some clouds and sure there would be a vivid picture on the other side. With her broad forehead and greeny-grey eyes, her rather broad nose and cleft chin, she struck him again as being handsome rather than beautiful. At last, she went on: 'He was worried. He spent a lot of time brooding. He was almost afraid of what he was going to find out: afraid of what he feared, if that makes any sense.' She looked up into Commyns' face, and demanded: 'Does it?'

'I think so,' said Commyns. 'The Farenza was planning something which made him fear that they could openly defy the police. But you have no idea what was being planned?'

'Not yet,' Felicity replied. 'Not yet.'

'But if you don't know now how can you possibly hope to find out?' asked Commyns. He did not speak testily but quite rationally, and he held her gaze all the time. 'Or don't you seriously hope to?' he asked at last. 'Is your "not yet" just wishful thinking?'

Her expression puzzled him. It was appraising yet there was a touch of impatience in it; long-suffering, perhaps. She folded her hands in her lap. The odd fancy, that she was like a seer trying to see into a crystal ball, returned more vividly. He had never met a woman like her. Suddenly she leaned forward and touched his arm, as if anxious to make him understand what she meant.

'Neil,' she said, 'I've come to know Pat better than I think

67

anyone else can, but there are gaps in my comprehension. Wide gaps, too. And although the Farenza has been on his mind for a long time, other things have preoccupied him simultaneously. It's no use telling you about irrelevant things. I have to search my mind and be sure I'm not misleading you.'

'Felicity . . .' Commyns began.

'No,' she protested, 'let me finish. I have had a very disturbed few days. I'm tremendously relieved tonight, but my mind isn't really clear. And I've got to think hard and examine all the things Pat has said lately and see if I can get them in the right context and perspective. That's what I mean when I say I haven't *yet* any idea what the Farenza was planning, and which worried Pat so. I might have a flash of understanding in an hour's time, or tomorrow while we're at the mock funeral – any time in fact. What I won't get is a response to direct questions or to pressure.' She pressed his arm again and added earnestly, perhaps pleadingly, 'Do you understand?'

'I understand fully,' Commyns said, in a most convincing voice. 'And I also understand that's time for me to go!' He got up in a long, slow movement, and she rose, too; she was half a head shorter. 'Thank you for everything,' he went on. 'May I call for you tomorrow?'

'Please,' she said. 'Just after eleven o'clock.'

'I shall be here,' promised Commyns, and he shook hands.

As Commyns went out of Dawlish's flat, Violetta Caselli was in her living-room, handing some mocha coffee to a small elderly man who had just come to see her. He had wiry grey hair and a craggy face, and she had known him ever since she could remember as Uncle Enrico. She was not sure whether he had come simply on a social visit or whether he had come as a messenger. She thought there was anxiety in his deep-set, pale brown eyes.

'It is very sad,' he said, 'the death of a good man. And when one reads the newspapers one does realize that this Dawlish was good. The funeral is tomorrow, then – at the Golders Green crematorium.' He gave a little shudder. 'I do not like cremations,' he said. 'I hope no one will cremate me. I want to think of these bones lasting for a long, long time.'

Soon he got up.

Soon she was alone.

All she could think about was whether she should go to the funeral of the man she had come to love.

CHAPTER NINE

GREAT OCCASION

THERE were thousands in and near the small crematorium: old friends of Dawlish in uniform, old friends in civvies, uniformed policemen and plainclothes. There were eleven men and women who had known Dawlish in the days when he had dropped by parachute behind the Nazi lines to sabotage communications and to help escaped prisoners who were in desperate need. Six were from France, three from Belgium, one from Denmark and one from Holland. They flew over at short notice, in deep distress.

There was no pomp and no ceremony.

The streets were thronged with people, all silent and grave; this was no peepshow. They had come to mourn a man whom all had known. Some of them had fought alongside him for years. There were the many he had helped, some whose lives he had saved; and there were the children, adults now, who were here because their parents had revered Patrick Dawlish as they had revered no one else in their lives.

The Home Office was represented.

So was the Queen.

So was Dawlish's regiment: The Guards.

So were men from the Civil Defence and the Fire Service; and so were newspapermen from all over the world. These were together in a space cordoned off and marked 'Press Only'. They had television reporters and radio reporters among them, all standing in a tense hush when eventually the coffin was brought in, carried by two uniformed and two plain-clothes detectives.

Felicity followed, with close friends – Ted Beresford and Toby Faringham and their wives.

In the Press enclosure old and young men marvelled.

'I'd no idea he was *this* well known.'

'What made him such a public hero?'

'How did they get here in time?'

'My God! What a man he must have been!'

And soon they were watching and photographing Felicity, who was dry-eyed but very pale, in a black coat and a black hat. In the event, Commyns had kept well behind, not having expected so many relatives and realizing that Felicity had made him welcome only because he had represented the Crime Haters. Commyns came in the car behind Gordon Scott's, whose face was pale and strained, and who did not look about him, except occasionally at Felicity.

Commyns looked everywhere.

He took in the Press enclosure, judged by the number there how widespread the publicity for this would be. He was surprised, even astonished, by the multitude in their obvious reverence. He saw the many who stood close to the gates of the crematorium and those who stood silently outside the chapel: and he noticed especially one woman who was near the front of the crowd. She could have gained that position only because she had arrived very early and waited here, for new arrivals were all being guided to the back.

It was a pleasant day, but not really warm.

The woman wore a dark cloth coat, but no hat. Her glossy black hair was well groomed and cut in a style more Italian than English. She was olive-skinned and very beautiful. Beautiful, Commyns thought, not handsome. She had a broad face and the rounded features of the south, and as he walked past her he saw that her dark eyes, chestnut-brown eyes, were stained with tears.

He thought: Who is she? Why is she so upset?

He wondered: Does Dawlish have a mistress?

He wondered again when he came out after the quick and simple ceremony, for the woman was in the same position, and he thought her a tragic figure.

Why?

He drew apart from the crowd and stood behind and

watched her. Hundreds of people were jostling now, but none took any notice of this woman. She moved at last towards the Garden of Remembrance, and for the first time he saw her take a little posy from a plastic handbag she had held by her side, and wait; and when the thousands had paid homage and the flowers were massed on great platforms, spreading high and wide, she dropped her posy with them and at last turned and hurried away.

Commyns began to follow her, but a group of men who had been standing at a distance suddenly moved towards the bank of flowers, and cut her off from him. There were too many for him to push through, and no chance at all to hurry. When at last he reached the gates she had disappeared among the crowd now slowly drifting away.

An hour later he was at Dawlish's office, with Gordon Scott, an elderly man named Childs – until recently Dawlish's right-hand man – and two others of the department. Dawlish 'had been' the Deputy Assistant Commissioner of the Criminal Investigation Department at New Scotland Yard, but that had been a rank created for him when the International Police Convention had been formed and he had been wanted as the British delegate. It was, to all intents and purposes, a separate department, with close liaison with the C.I.D. and the Special Branch, but with a great deal of autonomy. There were two huge counters, sloping downwards from adjoining walls, and a relief map of the world in Mercator Projection was spread here, not unlike the walls at the Celestia Travel Agency.

There was one great difference.

Tiny pinpricks of light showed whenever agents from the rest of the world wanted to make direct contact with him. Commyns saw the dot beneath Chicago; dots all over the world. Some were flashing on and off, but the calls were being answered in another room, not here. On shelves on a third wall was a mass of telegrams and cables and Gordon Scott was looking through these in a preoccupied, rather forlorn fashion. Commyns, watching the man, realized afresh how deeply he was troubled, how much he felt Dawlish's 'death'.

Only a handful of men knew the truth, and even now Commyns wondered whether the decision had been right.

Some kind of replacement would be necessary, many would think it must be permanent, others would want it to be temporary. As far as he could judge, however, everything was ticking over well. The pink elderly man, Childs, who looked consumptive, picked up a telephone on which a light glowed, and spoke for a moment, then put the receiver down and looked across at him, Commyns. He raised a frail hand, and smiled, Commyns moved across.

'It's for you,' Childs said, 'Mrs. Dawlish.'

'Thank you, Commyns said, and took up the receiver. 'Hallo, Felicity,' he went on in a subdued voice. 'I hope you're taking some rest.'

'Yes,' Felicity said, 'but there are some relatives here whom I'd very much like you to meet. Are you free to come to the flat?'

'Of course,' Commyns said, 'I'll be right over.'

His heart began to beat fast, for he knew that Felicity did not want him to meet her relatives, she wanted to talk to him but could not speak freely over the telephone. He crossed to Gordon Scott, who was shaking hands with an elderly man who had been at the funeral; before Commyns reached them, the elderly man went out. Scott was frowning; if he went on like this, Commyns thought, he would do more harm than good.

'Will you need me again, Gordon?'

Scott said: 'I shall probably need a lot of help before long. I've just been told that I'm to deputize for Mr. Dawlish until some more permanent arrangement can be made.'

'It could be a wonderful opportunity,' Commyns congratulated. He braced himself. 'One trouble is that I shall have to stay in London for a while although I'd much rather be in Rome.'

'There is probably a London end to this business,' said Commyns. 'Didn't Dawlish ever suggest that to you?'

'No,' Scott answered. 'There was something on his mind, but he didn't tell me.' He looked hard at Commyns and the hurt and bitter expression faded. 'He's much more likely to have given Mrs. Dawlish a hint. She could read him like a book. Will you try to find out if she knows anything that might help?'

'If I get a chance,' Commyns promised.

Scott gave a sudden, fierce grin. 'Walls have ears and eyes in this place,' he said, 'You'll be seeing Mrs. Dawlish in half an hour or so. This might not be the time to tackle her, but there's a good chance she'll have something to tell you.' The grin became positively aggressive. 'Let me know if she has, won't you?'

Commyns said helplessly: 'Yes, of course.'

'Thanks,' said Scott. 'You'll have to excuse me, there's a call from Sofia coming through.' He moved to a desk behind the big one where Dawlish usually sat. Childs was on a chair nearby, smiling faintly, giving the impression that he knew Commyns had been taken aback by Scott's aggressiveness.

He had come dangerously close to underrating Gordon Scott.

He went downstairs and on to the Embankment, let an empty taxi pass and began to walk to Millbank, not knowing that this had been Dawlish's favourite walk for years. A stiff breeze was coming off the Thames, and a spit of rain moistened the air. He glanced up at Big Ben; it was nearly three o'clock. By five past he was entering the building where the Dawlish penthouse was. The lift hustled him up. Three elderly women and an elderly man, all dressed in black, were leaving the penthouse, and Felicity was at the door.

As they went down, she and Commyns stood in the hallway.

'I've remembered something,' she told him with absolute certainty.

'I hoped you had.'

'There are a dozen people inside but if you say you have an important message for me from Rome they'll know we have to talk in private.'

'I'll do just that,' Commyns promised.

He had a feeling, started in a way by Gordon Scott, that instead of being the catalyst to what had happened, he was being pushed around; a pawn in a game started by Dawlish. There was a subdued babble of voices when he went in from people who were standing holding glasses and plates. An elderly silver-haired woman who looked remarkably like Felicity, came up.

'Mother,' Felicity said, 'I told you about Captain Commyns.'

'I am *very* glad you came last night,' Felicity's mother said.

'Captain Commyns has some things he must talk to me about,' said Felicity. 'Will you tell everyone, dear?'

'And I shall try to get them away soon,' the older woman said, and Commyns thought ruefully that he wasn't the only one being manipulated. He followed Felicity along the passage past a bathroom to a small bedroom which had an easy chair and a dressing-table.

'Do sit down,' Felicity said. She closed the door and sat on the bed with her legs doubled beneath her. He had never seen her face more vitally alive. 'I have remembered something which may be very pertinent.'

'Yes?' Commyns' voice was taut.

'There was a woman at Golders Green this morning whom I've seen before,' Felicity said. 'I was with Pat driving along the Strand about three weeks ago. He noticed and pointed to a woman coming out of a travel agency, and I'm quite sure the same woman was at the crematorium. I don't know her name, I don't know anything about her, but I do know that Pat was very intense. I made the remark "Is she a Farenza agent?" in the jesting way I told you about. He didn't deny it or reply in kind, just gave me an odd look. Then the woman disappeared into another shop.'

'Do you remember which one?'

'Oh yes – the Celestia Travel Agency, not far from Coutts Bank, opposite Charing Cross Station. And' – Felicity slipped her hand to the shallow neck of her dress and took out some folds of paper – 'I found these in one of Pat's suits this morning. It was the first time I've felt I could go through his clothes.'

She handed the papers over. They were travel brochures on shiny paper, and when he selected one he saw the Celestia Travel Agency printed across a galaxy of stars with a globe beneath it. He unfolded the brochure, with its glowing promises of package tours and golden sunshine, ships and sea and sand. Below it was a printed legend, of allied agencies in other parts of Europe. One made Commyns draw in a deep breath, for it read:

Euro-Economique Transport Cie – Ghent, Belgium.

'What is it?' exclaimed Felicity.

Commyns said: 'A Euro-Economique van was involved in an accident in Rome when two men we were after were killed. That's almost too much for coincidence. Have you any idea whether the woman works at the travel agency or was a client?'

'None,' Felicity said.

'Or any idea why she was at the funeral?'

'None,' Felicity said, 'except . . .'

'Go on,' Commyns urged.

'She looked very upset,' remarked Felicity, and he wondered whether she had the same thought as he: that Dawlish might have had a mistress. 'Did you notice?'

'Yes,' he said. 'And I saw her drop a tiny posy of flowers on to the others.'

Felicity sat very still and Commyns thought: She knows what it could mean. She sat in a most queenly way, casual as she was. Slowly a smile stole into her eyes, but there was compassion too.

'She wouldn't be the first woman to have fallen in love with Pat,' she remarked. 'He has an almost hypnotic appeal. And when he thought it would help he used it shamelessly.' She stared into Commyns' eyes, her expression unfathomable. 'You have that same kind of attraction for women, haven't you?' Before he could recover from his surprise and make even a muttered disclaimer, she went on: 'Shouldn't you try to use it with this woman?'

Commyns looked at Felicity very straightly, then began to smile; and his smile broadened as he said: 'I should be sorry for the man you tried your attraction on, if you weren't fond of him! Perhaps I should.' He slid a pencil out of one pocket and a slim notepad out of the other, got up and sat on the bed beside her, and began to sketch. In a few deft strokes he drew a woman's face, filled in an outline of her hair, and then her neck and shoulders. When he had finished he put his head on one side, appraising the likeness.

'About right?' he asked.

'It's very like the woman I saw,' declared Felicity, in surprise. 'Why, it's almost uncanny!'

75

'A man must have some talents,' said Commyns lightly. 'Now we'll see how long Gorden Scott will take to find out whether she works at Celestia or only visits.'

CHAPTER TEN

MEETING

'SHE works at the Celestia Travel Agency,' Gordon Scott told Commyns on the following afternoon. 'Her name is Violetta Casselli. She is an interpreter and speaks at least five languages, her native Italian, Spanish, French, English and German. She has worked at Celestia for three years, since the agency was opened. The manager is an Italian named Galli, Mario Galli, who is also the manager of a group of Celestia agencies in Britain – there is another in Manchester, one in Glasgow and one in Cardiff. All the senior officials are Italian, and have work permits – the parent company in Milan finances them all.' Scott was not reading from a list but sitting at the desk next to Dawlish's, looking at Commyns as he made the report. 'Galli is also the General manager of the Euro-Econ-omique Transport Company which has depots in all the major English seaports and the major airfields, but isn't registered in Britain. The trading figures for the transport company aren't yet known. The figures for the travel agency are very peculiar.'

Scott paused, obviously inviting a question. Commyns asked the obvious one.

'How peculiar?'

'It can't possibly make a profit out of the tours it books.'

'Are you sure?'

'We had a tax officer go and examine the books. Their cash-ier accountant has an office on the top floor of the building, and had to show them. The agency has the ground floor, Mario Galli's offices are on the first floor, the general offices are at the top.' Scott paused, before going on almost smugly: 'They are remarkable offices, too. Galli had a teleprinter connection with each allied office, and there are over fifty throughout the world, mostly in Europe and the United States. There are some indications that Celestia has associates in other countries with other names. Euro-Economique certainly has. It is a shipping and road delivery company, registered . . .'

Commyns could not resist interrupting.

'In Ghent.'

'That's right,' Scott agreed, unperturbed. 'It moves household goods and furniture mostly, but also some heavy machinery and some canned and bottled goods. It's genuine enough.'

'Does it make a profit?' asked Commyns dryly.

'I don't know why,' said Scott, blandly, 'but we haven't all the details yet.'

'Do you know how many Italians are involved?' asked Commyns.

'There's a fairly widespread Italian participation,' said Scott. 'But no greater than the American participation.'

'American!' exclaimed Commyns.

'Every piece of notepaper yet seen has shown at least one U.S. director,' Scott reported. 'And at least one of a European nationality.' He moved across the room and picked up some photographs, bringing them back to Commyns. 'These were taken today.' They were coloured snapshots of Violetta Caselli and each one was enough to make the average man widen his eyes, she was so strikingly lovely. 'I've checked among our people who were at the funeral; about twenty remember her.'

'Not surprising,' said Commyns. 'I wonder why she was there?'

'Nearly crying,' Scott remarked.

'Sure, that's right.'

'Captain . . .' Scott began.

'Neil,' corrected Commyns, quietly.

Scott hesitated, then gave a quick smile.

'Thank you. I was going to say that we need someone to find out why she was there, and we need to know soon. We're having her watched, of course.' His eyes were very direct. 'Do you feel like trying?'

'By now I'm pretty well known,' said Commyns. It was more comment than an objection.

'So was Pat Dawlish,' Scott observed. 'There's no doubt about her feeling for him.' After a pause he went on: 'We have a great deal of information about her already. There isn't much doubt that Pat knew much more.' It was obvious that he was unused to calling Dawlish 'Pat'. 'And no doubt we need to know more urgently.'

Commyns said: 'Did you know that a tape Dawlish made had been stolen from Salvatori's office?'

Scott went stiff as a statue.

'No,' he almost barked. 'I'd no idea. I ...' He gulped. 'I couldn't understand him leaving nothing behind. It wouldn't surprise me if there isn't another tape or sheaf of notes somewhere. He kept his reasoning to himself but when he had facts about what he thought, or valid conclusions, he always put them on record. Do you realize' – Scott's gaze was a glare and his words came out with great deliberation – 'that if it weren't for Pat Dawlish we would know practically nothing about the Farenza even now? There's a world-wide organization hell-bent on crime, and until recently no police force gave it serious thought.' When Commyns stayed silent, Scott demanded roughly: 'Did you know much about it?'

'No, except as a kind of Lodge,' Commyns confessed. 'The first I knew was when I met Salvatori and Pierre-Jacques in Rome.'

'And until Dawlish alerted them they didn't really know a thing,' growled Scott. 'Now we know that it's not only widespread, it can be deadly. Have you ever counted how many people were involved directly or indirectly in Pat's death? At least four and probably more, certainly more if you add the driver of the Euro-Economique truck and his mate.'

'I'll go along with that,' Commyns said calmly. 'The Farenza looks big and we have plenty to find out. And you want me to try to work on this Violetta Casselli.' He looked at the photographs, spread on a coffee table close to him; and he could picture her, pale and damp-eyed, at the crematorium. 'What you are really suggesting is that I act as ghost for Dawlish.'

'I wish to God *I* could!' exclaimed Gordon Scott.

'Can't you?' challenged Commyns, suddenly aggressive.

Scott opened his mouth to speak and closed it again, pursed his lips and gave Commyns as direct a stare as any man could. He was in his middle thirties, Commyns judged, perhaps even younger. There was great solidity about him and he had proved his competence, but there was something else which came through: a recognizable sense of integrity.

'No,' he said flatly. 'I'm not good enough.'

Commyns was completely taken aback.

'Listen, Gordon . . .'

'To do any job in the footsteps of Patrick Dawlish you have to be something very special,' Scott went on. 'I'm not that kind of special, and you know it. I might become the world's best second-in-command but that's as high as I'll ever go. You . . .' He began to walk about the room, looking at Commyns all the time. 'You've got something extra. You've a kind of Dawlish quality. You're the only man I know who could follow in his footsteps. I'm sure of one thing: if you're half as dedicated as he was, you'll try, whatever the cost.'

Commyns felt a strange warm glow, for this man meant exactly what he said. He hero-worshipped Dawlish but that did not blind him to what he saw, or believed he saw, in another. Commyns had a spasm almost of rage, that Scott should be one of those deceived about Dawlish's death, but for the first time he felt the wisdom of that. If Gordon Scott knew the truth it would show through. He would never say a word, never give a hint deliberately, but – gaiety would sing inside him and anyone observing him would know why.

'I think you rate me too high,' Commyns replied soberly. 'But I guess you don't give me any choice. Sure, I'll try.'

Scott's eyes gleamed as he said: 'You can count on me for anything, but you know that,' and then he clenched his hands and cried: 'Oh *God*! I wish he weren't dead!'

Commyns could not meet his gaze, but had to turn away.

In Dawlish there was awareness of light, pale light. That was all. He had no feeling, no sense of being alive, just of light. And a faint sound. He did not know that it was the sound of men's voices.

Violetta was aware of being followed.

She had felt this awareness before, with Patrick Dawlish. He would be standing on the other side of a street, or would jump down from a bus as she stood in a queue, or look at her from the window of a taxi. At any time while she was finding out what she could about him, he might suddenly appear out of the blue. Usually, he would smile. It wasn't a broad smile, his lips hardly parted and his teeth did not show. But his broken nose wrinkled! This caused rather a droll expression, lips curling and etching lines in the corner of his mouth. Often the smile had shown in his eyes. She had never seen eyes of such piercing blue – cornflower blue, the blue of the tiny flower as common in Italy as in England. She had thought for a while that he was enchanted by her. Could that be true? Or was he interested in her because of the Farenza? Was he interested in her for the same reason as she was in him? For her task was to probe into his activities, into anything he had done to probe the secrets of the Farenza. She, perhaps, more than anyone else, had known how far Dawlish had penetrated into the 'family'. Each time he had drawn closer to some central figure in the Farenza she had been fearful for him, knowing that one day he would be killed. His only hope was to stop his activity against the organization.

Just before the attacks on him began he had flown to Paris and broken into the home of the French leader of the Farenza and searched it. Whether he had found documents of importance she did not know. She did know that the news had gone through the organization like an electric shock.

Galli had sent for her, and said: 'None of us is safe from this man for as long as he lives.'

The words had slashed into her mind like a thrusting knife. The decision to kill him had been inevitable, and she had wondered why they had delayed so long.

'We would prefer not to challenge the Crime Haters openly,' Galli had said, making the reason so obvious. 'It is the only police organization in the world which thinks with one mind and acts as one. And Dawlish is their eyes and ears.'

Blind eyes now; and deaf ears.

Ten days ago she had watched his coffin being carried into the chapel, and had dropped quick-dying anemones as near his ashes as she could. Today for the second time she was aware of being followed, and in an uncanny way it was as if Dawlish had come back to life in another man's body.

This man was as tall as Dawlish. He had a harder, leaner, hungrier look, but there was the same kind of expression at his lips and eyes. Those eyes were greeny-grey, not cornflower blue, but just as piercing and bright. He would appear when she least expected it: out of shop doorways, on buses, as she turned corners. So far, he hadn't spoken to her. He must have appeared ten or twelve times, as if to haunt her.

She knew that Mario Galli realized she was on edge, but believed he put that down to her distress over Dawlish. She should have told him about this other man, but had not yet been able to bring herself to do so. She knew it was necessary because the Farenza demanded it but she did not want to play any part which would lead to the death of another man. She felt more than ever responsible for Dawlish's death, and the hurt and sense of guilt and remorse grew stronger.

Today was Sunday.

She had slept late, after taking a sleeping pill, had break-fasted lazily, washed her smalls and ironed her sheets and pillow-cases, then had gone out of the apartment house. Old Benvenuti, who lived round the corner, was walking towards her with the Sunday newspapers.

'*Buon Giorno*,' he said, smiling.

'*Buon Giorno,* Benvenuti.'

She walked on. A short but handsome young man, obviously Italian, came out of a house, and she knew it was no accident, he timed such an encounter often.

'*Giorno*.'

'*Buon Giorno,* Danelli,' she smiled mechanically.

'Will you have lunch with me today, Violetta?'

'You are very kind,' she said, 'but I have an appointment for lunch.'

'All the time, these appointments,' he complained. 'I do not believe in them. Am I not as handsome as he?'

'I don't know anyone better-looking than you,' she soothed.

He walked with her to Kensington High Street, and waited with her for a bus. She had no plans, except to go to St. James's Park where she loved the lake and the birds and the flowers. There would be great beds of daffodils today, the long buds had started to open last week. A bus came along and Danelli put a hand to her elbow.

'Next week, Violetta, *please*.'

'Perhaps next week,' she replied, and his dark eyes lit up.

The sun was beginning to break through low clouds and it was warmer than it had been for the past few days. This was a morning for a long ride, and if the front seat at the top were empty she would go to the terminal, somewhere in North London, and come back to the park. The bus was moving by the time she got on top, but there *was* a front bench free! She swayed and staggered towards it and dropped down. The sun shone suddenly bright on a terrace of tall houses, and into the bus. She felt warm and relaxed. A young Negro conductress, her face shiny black and her eyes like stars, came up to her.

'All the way, please.'

The ticket machine went *ting*! There was no change out of a two-shilling – ten pence, she must remember! – piece. She was aware of people coming on to the bus, there was a continual sense of movement. The front bench across the aisle from her was taken by a man and two small boys, who glued their noses to the window. Inevitably a man came and sat by her side, and she edged closer to the window but did not look round. He had beautifully polished brown shoes and narrow trousers, adjusted just above the ankle. He had a lean, tanned brown hand which rested on his left leg, and his arm was close to hers; sometimes as the bus swayed at a curve he was thrust against her or she against him. For a long time she watched the road ahead, the traffic, the sidewalks which were not busy but on which some always walked, giving a swiftly changing scene.

Then she looked up at him.

It was the man who was like, yet unlike, Dawlish.

Quite deliberately and very slowly he took her gloved hand in his and squeezed gently. At the same moment he smiled more widely. He had good, white teeth, two of them capped with gold.

'Hallo,' he said, and she knew he was an American. 'I've wanted to talk to you for a long time.'

'Please . . .' she began.

'I am a friend of Patrick Dawlish,' he stated simply.

She caught her breath and her colour began to ebb from her cheeks.

'I – I do not know who you mean.'

'Then why were you at his funeral?' he asked.

She swallowed hard. 'I do not know.'

'Violetta,' he interrupted, 'we have to talk, and you have to tell me all you can. For we are both friends of Dawlish. I want you to come with me to a place where we can talk quietly, and where you need not be afraid. Please.' He drew her towards him and she could not resist, was moved by a compulsion she did not understand, to go with him. He let her go ahead, and kept a hand on her shoulder to help steady her, even as they went down the stairs. They were in Knightsbridge, across the street from Harrods. Only a few people were on the sidewalk; no one waited at the bus-stop, but two at a car which drew up behind the bus.

The man got off, and helped her down.

Without the slightest warning he flung his arms round her and thrust her close to a brick wall built to guard the roadway from the higher pavement. She heard three sharp reports. She felt a shower of chipping. This man's face was above her and his lean body was heavy on hers. A woman screamed; men began to shout, and the man above her got up slowly, helped her up, and then stared along the street. Some way off, two men rushed back to the car, but were stopped by others who appeared in yet another car, behind it. They turned and began to run – two dark-haired men.

The car which had already impeded them now raced towards them. Another car came swinging across the traffic and men leapt from it. Now the pair who were running had men close behind them and others in front. One of the fugitives made a wild leap into the road, and as he did so a car, travelling too fast, smashed into him. The other man who had been running stood and stared at the awful sight, while those in front and those behind closed in on him.

That was the moment when Violetta realized that the prisoner was Danelli, who had pleaded with her to go to lunch with him.

'Violetta,' said the tall American, now helping her up, 'It is time you decided who are your friends and who are your enemies. Those two men tried to kill you.'

CHAPTER ELEVEN

THE PRISONER

THERE had been few people about; suddenly there were dozens, soon there were hundreds, old and young, white and black, well dressed and shabby. But the only faces Violetta could see were of the man who now stood with an arm about her, protectively – and Danelli's. Danelli now had his back to her. He stood between a policeman whose helmet towered high above the round black head, and a man in an ordinary suit and dark hair with a very white bald patch, like a friar's. They were close to a car, the door of which was opened by another policeman. Danelli was pushed inside.

How had he got here?

Why had the police arrested him?

She lifted her head, and found the tall man looking down on her. His lips opened to make some comment. He closed them again, and his eyes held a startled expression. His arm tightened about her waist.

There were more people and more policemen, two of these out in the road, directing traffic. Opposite was the huge browny-red building she knew well: Harrods. Above, the blue sky. About her, the voices of the people in the crowd. Then she had a mental picture of what had happened and she realized that one of the men who had lurked in the doorway had been Danelli.

A policeman began to call: 'Gangway, please – gangway . . .' He and another forced people back, made a path between her and her companion and the roadway. The man's arm was very firm and reassuring about her. She felt numbed, for she knew one thing which she did not want to admit.

At the kerb stood a large car with its doors open.

Danelli had shot at her.

The tall man who had followed her about so much of late said: 'Get in, honey.'

Danelli had tried to kill her.

She sat in the far corner, and the man had to bend double as he joined her. From behind, a man asked:

'Did you say Millbank, Mr. . . .'

Her companion replied, sharply: 'Yes. Just beyond Lambeth Bridge.'

'Very good, sir.'

Or had Danelli tried to shoot this man?

The thought brought a whirl of relief, lightening her heart, her breast, her whole body coursing like wine through her veins to her hands and feet, making her feel momentarily as if she could fly.

Danelli had not tried to kill her but to kill this man.

Outside, a policeman was holding traffic back, and pushing people away. A man with a narrow face and deep, shadowed eyes was very close to her. She thought she had seen him before. Then the car moved off, and she sat very still, feeling better than she had but without that sensation of exhilarating relief. She stared straight ahead, past the driver's head. Everything in front of her was normal again: a few people, a few cars, a few buses, buildings so tall she could not see the top, traffic lights. She sensed that her companion was looking at her but she did not glance round.

At last he said: 'You know they tried to kill you, don't you?' When she didn't answer he went on in his rather attractive way: 'I guess it follows that I saved your life.' When she still didn't answer he went on as if he were laughing to himself: 'If you think I put your life in danger, maybe that makes us even.'

She turned her head and said with great intensity: 'They did not try to kill me, they tried to kill you.' For a few moments she stared up at him in defiance, but his return gaze was so disconcerting that she looked away quickly. They were approaching the underpass beneath Hyde Park Corner, and suddenly they were inside it, the tyres roaring and the noise echoing, the lights on either side like the cold eyes of a huge reptile reflecting but not creating life. She thought: *Danelli did not try to kill me, he tried to kill this man.*

She repeated that to herself time and time again as if it were a lifeline she must clutch unless she wanted to sink and die.

Neil Commyns did not think there was a woman alive who could fool him; not a woman alive who could make him take his mind off his job. But as he looked down at Violetta Casselli's face it was like looking down at a Botticelli angel. Of doom.

There was such grief in her eyes: grief and shock.

Her features were flawless, as he had known since he had first seen her at close range, but the emotions aroused this morning touched that beauty with a golden light; the emotions and the lamps they passed. Gradually the daylight strengthened and the tunnel fell behind them, but the grief remained. Violetta sat with her hands folded in her lap. She wore a dress which was neither brown nor gold, but somewhere between, trimmed with dark brown. The hem fell just above her knees; demurely. She sat so still that he did not really want to disturb her, but he must. He did not want to shake her out of her tense calm, but he must. He did not want to shock her into accepting the truth, but he had to.

'The two men followed you all the way from your home,' he stated flatly. 'Danelli Fenelli went with you, Luigi Fenelli was behind him in a car which was parked near the bus stop, and followed the bus. I know because at that stage I was in a car which followed them.'

He paused, to give her time to take this in. She showed no sign of having heard, but she must have done. They were in Green Park now, the Palace with its iron-spike-protected wall on one side, the tree-clad grassland on the other. The great gates, gilded and shiny black, stood on one side: Buckingham Palace and the statue of Queen Victoria facing it.

Neil was aware of all this, but looked only at Violetta's profile.

'They still followed when I drove ahead of the bus, left my car and came to join you, and then they stayed close behind until we began to get off. I had another car following them, and they were quick enough to shoot but not quick enough to get away.'

She stared ahead, mute and still.

'And Danelli shot at you in cold blood,' Neil Commyns stated flatly.

At last she turned her head, and flashed: 'It is not true!'

'Every word is true.'

'Then how could they know when you were going to take me off the bus?'

'It is easy to see people as they start down the twisting staircase,' he answered. 'I have no doubt that we shall find binoculars in the car, which would have enabled them to be absolutely sure.'

For the first time she look nonplussed, and before long she looked afraid.

'They shot at you,' she insisted.

'They shot at you and hoped to get me, too.'

'They shot at *you*.'

'They wanted you first,' Neil said, harshness creeping into his voice. 'They would have caught up with me later, just as they caught up with Dawlish and killed him.'

Something happened to her. He thought it was physical as well as emotional shock which first stiffened her body and then made her shiver, next made her turn towards him as if her body had suddenly turned to liquid. She opened her mouth to speak, but words stuck on the tip of her tongue. Her eyes blazed momentarily, but almost at once the fire died, her body drooped, her lips quivered as if they would melt into tears.

And all this, Neil thought with new excitement, because she had heard him talk of Dawlish's death.

This was the first time that he was really convinced the decision to pretend that Dawlish was dead was the right one.

This was not the right moment to try to make her talk; she was at a high peak of emotional distress and needed help and understanding, not pressure which would increase her tension and perhaps forever make her hostile. They were near Parliament Square and in a few minutes would be at Dawlish's home. He saw the film of tears in her eyes, perhaps because she realized that. She looked out of the window, away from him, but he did not think she saw the Houses of Parliament, or, just beyond, the river, which was calm as a pond. Even when the car turned off the Embankment, and pulled up at the front of the great block of concrete and glass, did she seem to be aware of where she was.

She exclaimed: 'No!'

'Much better here than at a police station,' Neil Commyns said.

Soon, the girl beside him, the driver in the foyer behind him, he telephoned Felicity Dawlish, keeping his voice low. She answered at once.

'Felicity,' Neil said. 'You remember we talked about Violetta Casselli?'

'Of course I remember,' Felicity said.

'She is downstairs with me. Two of her friends tried to shoot her, and she's in some distress. Will you let me bring her up?'

Again, but in a different tone, Felicity said: 'Of course, Neil.'

'Fel,' he said.

'Yes?'

'She thinks Pat is dead.'

'Neil,' Felicity said, and he could have sworn there was a hint of laughter in her voice, 'I have been married to this kind of life for a long time.'

'Meaning, I don't have to stress the obvious,' Neil replied, and a responding chuckle echoed in his voice. 'You'll have to get used to it, honey, I always do stress the obvious. It's a very good insurance.'

'I see what you mean,' she said.

She thought: He's uncannily like Pat. He thinks like him, works like him. She meant that Pat would have brought this woman here, and would have reminded her, if in a different way, that she must not show by deed or word or attitude that she knew Pat was alive. As she prepared to let them in, she realized that the warning had been necessary. There was more: this woman might well have helped lead Pat to his death, and would think herself face to face with his widow.

Violetta felt the man's fingers on her arm, steadying her. She needed steadying, for she was trembling and her knees were quaking. That was from shock, of course, as well as the subconscious realization of the truth. Danelli *had* shot to kill her,

88

to silence her as the men in Rome had been silenced. Also it was the fact that she was going to come face to face with Dawlish's wife. Once or twice she had seen them together. Suddenly, the door opened and Mrs. Dawlish stood there, just as Violetta remembered, tall and distinguished and handsome. Her lips were set, her grey-green eyes cold, until she said:

'Come in.'

Neil Commyns ushered Violetta forward. Felicity stood to one side to let them pass. There was a passage to the right and another to the left, and straight ahead a beautiful room, very large and with huge windows, which met in one corner, showing the whole of London beyond. The windows created an illusion that the silhouette of the city was in fact a mural painted on a vast wall.

'Felicity,' Neil said, 'this is Violetta Casselli.' He turned to Violetta. 'Violetta, this is Mrs. Dawlish.'

Violetta said huskily: 'I know.'

'Come and sit down, and tell me what happened this morning,' said Felicity. She took the girl's arm and led her to a huge couch, covered in dark green, and looked up at Neil. Had he been Pat he would have known that this was a moment to leave her with Violetta. 'Neil, if you could make some coffee ...'

'Coffee coming up,' he said, and went into the kitchen; but he left the door open and soon there were the little noises: gas popping, china chinking, spoons rattling.

'Tell me what happened,' Felicity said.

After that first coldness of greeting there was warmth and understanding in her, and Violetta sensed it as she sat down. The couch was beautifully comfortable. She sank into it. Felicity Dawlish pulled up a velvet-covered pouffe which matched the couch, and sat down. There was something very natural in her manner.

'I – I do not really know,' Violetta said in a low-pitched voice. 'Your – your friend has been following me.' *Like your husband did*, she wanted to cry, but did not. 'He came on the top of a bus, and – and when we got off, we were – we were fired at.' *Like your husband was fired at on the Spanish Steps!* she wanted to scream, but she did not. 'And your – your friend saved me. He ...' She broke off and began to breath very heavily, fighting back tears. 'He says he did but *he* was to have been killed, they meant to shoot him, not me!' When Felicity made no comment, simply sat relaxed and looking at her gravely, Violetta cried: 'Danelli would not shoot me. He would not, I tell you. He would not shoot me!'

Felicity asked: 'Who is Danelli?'

'He is an old friend. I have known him since he was a little boy. He would not shoot me, I am sure of it!'

She was lying to herself. She had a vivid mind picture of what had happened and knew that Danelli had levelled his gun at her.

In sudden panic she began to say to herself: 'He wouldn't kill me, I know he wouldn't, he wouldn't kill me!' Then suddenly the tears began to flow. She did not know how it happened, but she felt this woman's arms about her, comforting, and for a while she did not realize how strange it was that Felicity Dawlish should comfort her. All she knew was that after a while she felt much better. Soon she was sitting with her legs upon the couch, a cushion behind her back, and Felicity had poured out coffee from a tray which stood on the pouffe. There was no sign of the man. She began to utter short, almost incoherent phrases.

'Sorry, very sorry, I didn't want them to kill him, I did not want them to, he was such a good man. Such a good man. And he was your husband. They killed him, please believe me! I did not wish it. I did not wish for him to die.'

'Violetta,' Felicity said gently, 'my husband knew the risks. Try to drink this, dear.'

Dear.

Violetta's hand trembled as she took the cup, but at last she sipped. It was hot, strong, sweet. She sipped again. A faint steam rose from the coffee and softened this woman's face, this widow's face. She sipped again. Tears rolled down her cheeks. She tried to speak but could not. When the coffee was gone, despite the tears she felt better. Felicity Dawlish handed her a crumpled handkerchief, and she dried her cheeks, then looked straight at the other woman and heard herself saying:

'I knew one day they would kill him. I – I hated them for it. I did not want him to die. I – I hated the thought of his dying. But it was inevitable, because he learned too much about them.' She spread her hands towards Felicity as if pleading.

'Not until after he was killed did I know it had been inevitable, while he was alive I lied to myself. And – and I helped them because I told them all I could about him. I helped them kill your husband! Do you understand?'

CHAPTER TWELVE

TWO WOMEN

'YES,' Felicity replied quite clearly. 'I do understand.'
'I helped them kill him!'
'Yes,' said Felicity again. 'I knew you had.'
'You – *knew*?'
'Many things are inevitable,' Felicity said. 'There is always a pattern.' She had the other's small, pale hands in hers. She felt a great sorrow for her and there was an almost overwhelming temptation to tell her that Pat was not dead, it would help her so. She knew, now, how she could win the girl's confidence, and that was the vital need. The situation was so delicate that one false word could destroy the illusion of grief, of sorrow; and the only way to maintain the illusion without seeming hard and callous was the way of understanding. So she went on: 'There *is* always a pattern. Pat was a policeman and he always took risks; one day the risk was bound to be too great.'
'You do not – hate me?'
Felicity tightened her grip a little and looked straight into Violetta's eyes. 'Why should I hate you?'
'But I helped to kill him!'
'Not you,' Felicity said. 'The organization, yes, I hate that. But you – what else could you do but obey?'
Violetta exclaimed: 'There was nothing I could do!'
'No,' agreed Felicity. 'The organization told you what to do, as it tells all of its members, and the day came when you became dangerous to them because you had obeyed them: so, the time came when you had to die, too.' Felicity paused, then

released Violetta, and asked in a brisker voice: 'More coffee?'

'How is it you understand so much?'

'I have been a policeman's wife for a long time. Pat did not hate all the individuals, he had great compassion for most. But he hated the organization.' She hesitated, and then went on: 'The Farenza.'

Violetta gasped: 'You know the name?'

'He had known it for months.'

'But it is a secret name!'

'Policemen learn secrets,' Felicity said. 'Violetta, what are you going to do?'

'I – I do not understand you.'

'It is easy to understand,' Felicity replied quite matter-of-factly. 'You cannot go back to your home or your work, can you? They would have to kill you. The police – not even Neil Commyns, who brought you here – would be able to protect you at either place.'

'Why should he protect me?' Violetta demanded.

'Because it is his job,' Felicity answered simply. 'Now that you've been attacked all the policemen in London will try to protect you, but . . .'

'I cannot be safe,' Violetta interrupted. 'Once they have decided that I must die . . .' She broke off and shivered again; the coffee-cup shook in her hands. 'No one is safe when they are in danger to the Farenza.'

'Or become dangerous,' Felicity said in that matter-of-fact way. 'The Farenza, the Mafia, whatever the organization is, doesn't matter. They protect themselves only by violence and killing. That is why the police have to fight and try to smash them.'

Violetta said simply: 'No one can smash the Farenza. It is too strong.' Her eyes blazed suddenly. 'Don't you understand? They killed your husband, they will kill anyone who threatens them. No one is safe – no policeman, no politician, no – no one, not even those who have served it faithfully.'

Very carefully, Felicity said: 'It is evil. It has to be destroyed. I shall fight it until it has been destroyed or it destroys me.'

They looked intently at each other.

They were utterly unalike, the one so dark-haired and olive-skinned, the other so fair; one pair of eyes velvety dark, the other like the grey-green of the sea, lit by the sun. Violetta's lips were parted, she breathed heavily, as if in distress, but Felicity's composure was absolute.

They did not move; they seemed oblivious of everything but themselves, as if Neil Commyns was not in the flat and they were absolutely alone.

But he *was* in the flat, and he watched them and listened to them for what seemed a long time: marvelling.

Neil had never felt so strange.

He felt as if he were not himself but Dawlish; that Dawlish, not he, should be here, witnessing and overhearing this encounter between the two women who loved him. It did not seem absurd to Neil that he should think 'loved' him. The way Violetta had behaved when he had talked of Dawlish's death, her expression whenever Dawlish was mentioned, her expression now, convinced him of that. The belief that Dawlish was dead made anguish for her, as great an anguish as Felicity had felt when she had believed him dead.

What did Felicity feel for her, now?

He thought: Compassion; only compassion.

But there was more than compassion in her. There was a clear, cool, calculating mind working with great precision, bringing Violetta nearer and nearer to breaking point, despite all her loyalties, all her tradition. He watched Violetta's face as Felicity said with such care:

'It is evil. It has to be destroyed. I shall fight it until it has been destroyed or it destroys me.'

The anguish Violetta was suffering was naked in her face, especially in her eyes. Her lips began to quiver. Neil thought, with a touch of alarm, that she was being pushed too far, that she would easily be driven to defending the Farenza, and then he saw Felicity's expression change. She relaxed, and moved a little further away, then leaned forward and rested a hand reassuringly on Violetta's arm.

'How can we expect to see this the same way?' she asked. She stood up with a graceful movement surprising in so tall a woman. 'Will you forgive me if I offer one piece of advice?'

Huskily, Violetta said: 'It will be easy to forgive anything.'

'When Neil Commyns or any policeman questions you, tell the truth,' said Felicity. 'If there are things you can't tell them because you don't know, they will believe you if they know that what you do say is true. And if there are things you know but will not tell them, perhaps out of loyalty, let them know that, too.'

Neil thought, My God, she knows exactly what to say! He saw the effect of the advice on Violetta, the calming; and then he withdrew from the doorway, for Felicity turned towards the kitchen door, and her body hid Violetta. He had a flash thought, that Violetta should not be left alone, but the thought died. Had she been driven too far, then she might have tried to kill herself rather than be forced to betray the Farenza. Instead, she was calm.

Felicity was saying: 'I'm famished, and I'm sure you and Neil must be.' She spoke as if they were old friends. She pushed the kitchen door open and stepped inside, closed the door behind her, yet allowed it to spring open again, not latching. She lowered her voice, as if anxious that Violetta should not hear her, and said to Neil: 'She needs some rest, please don't question her yet.'

Neil, standing out of sight, said firmly: 'I shall have to talk to her soon.'

'But not yet,' Felicity pleaded.

He gave a funny little laugh, and said: 'All right.' Then he went on: 'I must check what happened with the others.' He paused, before adding: 'Did I hear you mention food?' He watched Dawlish's wife as he spoke, and again he had a strange feeling that he did not belong here; that he was living in another man's shoes.

'It will have to be eggs and bacon,' Felicity said, and then as if with inspiration: 'Do you think Violetta would like something Italian – I *could* provide spaghetti and meat balls!'

Neil was still chuckling when he went back to the living-room. Violetta stood looking out over London. Felicity followed Neil, went straight to her, and said: 'I'm sure you would like to tidy up,' and led her back through the kitchen to the spare bedroom. Their voices sounded for a few moments, before Felicity reappeared in the big room.

'You do know she's absolutely at the end of her tether, don't you?' she asked.

'Yes,' he answered.

'You couldn't leave her with me for the rest of the day, could you?' she might talk more freely if you could.'

Neil replied quietly: 'I'm not sure you're not too kind-hearted. May we talk about it later?'

'Yes, of course,' Felicity agreed.

Neil saw another change in her expression but could not understand it. There was relief, he thought, and perhaps a decision in the making. What would she decide now, beyond what they had agreed? He went slowly to the telephone which stood on a table near the door, with a winged armchair beside it, picked the instrument up, and dialled Scott's number: Dawlish's office number. The ringing sound went on for a long time: surely the office wouldn't be deserted, even on a Sunday. The *burr-burr* broke, and Gordon Scott answered.

'Deputy A.C.'s office.'

'Hi, Gordon,' Neil said.

'Hallo,' Scott said. There was something about him which made him seem very young. 'Very glad to hear you. Are you still with Mrs. Dawlish?'

'Yes.'

'If you don't mind me putting my oar in,' Scott said, 'She could get a lot out of the Casselli girl if you give her time.'

'That sounds like the other half of a conspiracy,' Neil said dryly. 'What's the news of the prisoner?'

'He won't say a word,' reported Scott. 'The dead one is named Luigi Fenelli, the other one Danelli Fenelli.'

'Brothers?'

'Cousins, according to neighbours. They live near Violetta Casselli. We have a team of our own people and the C.I.D. division over there,' Scott went on, and satisfaction showed in his voice. 'This is the first time we've been able to make any progress in that area. It's nearly solid Italian, with a few families from other European countries. It's like a big tribe living in the heart of London.'

'Quite a colony,' Neil remarked.

'Colony is a better word,' Gordon Scott agreed. 'We're searching the house where the Fenellis live, as well as Violetta

Caselli's apartment. This will give us a chance to go to her office – that's one thing I wanted to check with you, sir.' The 'sir' slipped out, nothing would convince Scott that he wasn't talking to a senior officer in his own organization. 'Shall we raid Celestia Travel now or wait until tomorrow when everyone's at his post, so to speak?'

'If you wait until tomorrow, someone might go and clean the place out,' objected Neil.

'I shouldn't worry too much about that,' Scott said, 'We've got it watched back and front and from windows in the building across the road, seven storeys higher. If anybody goes there, they won't get away with a thing.'

Neil found himself on the point of asking: 'What would Dawlish do?' Then he checked himself. If he were in Chicago and in command, what would *he* do? The temptation would be to keep the Celestia offices under surveillance, and pick up anyone who went there, even the genuine tourists; it would be too risky to let them go in.

He said so.

'Trouble with that is that we'd have to station someone very near, to prevent anyone from going in. Might warn 'em off,' Scott added briskly, 'but I'm sure you're right, and I'll fix it somehow.' He reflected for a moment before going on: 'One other thing, sir – unless you've got anything else.'

'What about Mario Galli?' Neil asked.

'The man who runs Celestia? He's under close watch at his home in Hampstead.'

'Do you know whether he knows about the shooting and the arrests?'

'There's no way of telling,' answered Scott. 'He could have had a dozen telephone calls. He hasn't had a visitor, or I would have been told.' Then Scott added in that naïve, youthful way Neil Commyns was getting to know so well: 'You can be sure he *knows*. They all know. They must have their own kind of tom-tom signals! They all know and they all keep their mouths shut. "I saw nothing, I heard nothing, I say nothing", that's the attitude.'

'Three wise monkeys,' Neil remarked dryly. 'Have you heard from a lawyer yet?'

'A who?'

'A lawyer. An attorney.'

'Oh, you mean has anyone turned up to represent the ac-cused? No,' went on Scott. 'He's ben charged with using an offensive weapon with intent to cause grievous bodily harm, and will be up at South-West Magistrates' Court in the morn-ing. We'll know whether he's going to be represented by then. If anyone turns up before, I'll let you know.'

'Thank you,' Neil said. 'What was it you were going to tell me?'

'I've had a call from General Salvatori,' Gordon Scott re-ported. 'He says that there is no news.'

In fact, Dawlish was now having spells of consciousness.

'Felicity ...' His voice was little more than a whisper. 'Felicity ...' And when a nurse leaned over him he said faintly: 'I want to see my wife.'

Neil Commyns turned away from the telephone, sat back and stared at the closed kitchen door. He did not know how long he sat – for ten or fifteen minutes, perhaps. He looked stern and set-faced, remembered saying to her that he was afraid she would be too kind-hearted, remembered also that Scott had said she could probably learn more than he could from Violetta. The kitchen door opened and Felicity stood there, quite gay-eyed and youthful-looking.

'Come and get it, as the Americans say,' she said lightly, and opened the door wide. 'Goodness! You're looking serious. You ...' She caught her breath, her expression changed, fear was like a vivid slash across it. 'It's not – Pat. He's not – worse?'

'No!' Neil said, almost sharply. 'No, I would tell you at once if he were.'

He was caught by surprise by her naked fear, the raw hurt in her, and realized for the first time how much she was living off her nerves and how cleverly and courageously she concealed it.

Then, without quite knowing what happened, he found him-self standing with his arms about her; felt her shoulders heav-ing, heard her gasping as if for breath: *sobbing*. All he could do was stand and hold her.

CHAPTER THIRTEEN

'SLEEP'

NEIL COMMYNS soothed Felicity as best he could. His right
hand strayed to her hair: soft, silky, touched with grey. His
fingers became buried in it. Her cheek was against his; he could
feel the dampness of her tears. He was acutely aware of her, as
a woman. He had known many women since his one disastrous
marriage but it was a long, long time since he had really been
stirred by one.

She was Dawlish's wife.

What the hell was the matter with him? She was Dawlish's
wife, suffering from delayed shock.

He was comforting her and exciting himself.

What seemed an age after he had begun to hold her, the
telephone bell rang. He felt Felicity's whole body stiffen, felt
her draw away. He said in a husky voice: 'I'll get it,' and freed
himself and crossed to the telephone which was ringing insist-
ently. He picked it up, keeping his back to Felicity so that she
could not see his expression. He was quivering and his voice
was unsteady.

'This is Neil Commyns.'

'Mr. Commyns, hold on, please. Mr. Scott would like a word
with you.'

Thank God for Scott! No interruption could have been
more timely. He held on, turning back. Felicity was on her way
to her bedroom, she also needed the respite. He felt a rumble in
his stomach and realized that he was famished – my God, how
could a man think of food in such circumstances?

'Sorry to keep you.' Scott was obviously in a hurry. 'Two
things, Neil.' He was much more sure of himself. 'Mario Galli,
the British manager – or, rather, manager for the United King-
dom of Celestia Travel – is at London Airport. He's just picked
up a ticket for Rome which was reserved under the name of

Mario Guilliano, and he's due to catch the four o'clock flight and will be boarding in ten minutes or so.'

'Passport?' asked Neil brusquely.

'We had a man at the Immigration desk – the passport was in the name of Guilliano.'

'And the question is, let him go to Rome or pick him up here?' Commyns asked.

'Exactly.'

'What do you think?'

'Hold him.'

'I'm with you all the way,' Neil said emphatically. 'I'd get him off that plane if I had to carry him.' Again it flashed through Commyns' mind that Scott was deferring to his judgment as if he, Neil Commyns, were in fact a superior, as if he considered him to be in charge. But that was absurd; he wasn't anything of the kind. 'What was the other thing?'

'General Salvatori is flying from Rome with Pierre-Jacques and Fernandez Lohn.'

'Another good reason for keeping Galli alias Guilliano here,' Neil said.

'I'll be in touch,' Scott cut his words short and rang off.

Neil moved towards the corner window and stared over that magnificent view yet was aware only vaguely of the loops of the Thames and a pale sunshine gleaming on the water. He was acutely conscious of the door opening, and Felicity coming in again, but wasn't sure whether she was approaching him or not. He actually clenched his teeth as he turned round. She was nearer the kitchen than the window.

'I'm sorry, Neil,' she said.

'*You've* nothing to be sorry about.'

'You've more than enough to do without having to cope with a prostrate female,' she said with enforced lightness. 'If you can eat bacon and eggs which have been keeping warm on a hot-plate, everything's ready.'

'And the spaghetti and meat balls?' He made an effort to be funny, too. 'What happened to them?'

'I didn't open the can!'

A small counter in the kitchen was set for two people. Bacon still sizzled, coffee burped and chuckled in a percolator. Cream and sugar, cups and saucers, were on a tray. Felicity took a

99

large electric frying pan off the stove and piled eggs and bacon, rather overdone, on to his plate.

'Isn't Violetta eating?' Neil asked.

'She's asleep.'

'*Asleep!*' echoed Neil. 'You mean . . .?' He slid off the stool and strode towards the door leading to the passage, then to one which led to the bedroom where Violetta was.

She lay on the bed, with a quilt over her. She was very pale and very still. He moved swiftly to her and put his fingers on her cool wrist; he could detect only a faint movement. He spun round on Felicity and there was roughness and accusation in his voice.

'You should have told me at once! She's drugged herself. If she should die . . .'

Felicity said very quietly: 'She didn't drug herself, and she won't die.'

Neil began: 'What the devil do you mean?' He broke off, suddenly becoming aware of what she meant. And just as a few minutes ago he had felt only deep compassion for an awareness of her, now he boiled with anger and did not trust himself to speak.

'I gave her sleeping pills,' Felicity said at last. 'She will be asleep for five or six hours.'

'What made you do such a crazy thing?' He had to fight not to shout.

'I don't think it was crazy.'

'It was crazy and it was' – now he fought for the stinging word, couldn't find it, and went on – 'bloody presumptuous.' Why the English 'bloody' came out he didn't know. He saw her go pale. 'Don't ever do anything behind my back again.'

She looked at him very levelly, only her eyes bright; and then she said in a hoarse voice: 'I'm sorry. I thought it was a good idea.'

That was the moment when he should have been gracious; when, whatever he felt, he ought to make peace. But he was still fuming inwardly and could not stop himself from rasping:

'You did it to stop me from talking to her! You bloody, interfering . . .'

He bit the word 'bitch' back, but too late. Her eyes looked

like glass, her lips tightened into a thin line; he thought she was going to speak, for they began to tremble, but instead she turned away. She went into the big room and the door swung to behind her. He stared unseeing at the congealing bacon and eggs, furious with himself, yet at the same time bitterly angry with Felicity. But he should have controlled himself, nothing gave him the right to call her out like that. Oh, what the hell! He went after her but she wasn't in the room. What the devil should he do? He went into the passage, and opened a door there. Violetta lay as if asleep.

Sight of her seemed to lay a soothing hand on him.

It was madness to have drugged her but he could compare her calmness now with her despair and distress before. And he saw her more beautiful than he had ever seen her, dark hair against the white pillow, skin more peach than olive, long, curved lashes, sharply defined eyebrows. She had needed rest, Felicity was right about that, but – she should now be answering questions, in her weakness she might have talked more freely. It had been madness . . .

He went out, reached the next door, and tapped.

'I'm sorry,' Felicity called. 'I don't feel like talking just now.'

He could believe that!

'All right,' he said. 'I'll get in touch later.'

But he didn't move away, didn't want to go. What could have made him lose his self-control so? Why did it matter that at this moment his heart was heavy and he felt the worst kind of a heel?

The least he could do was to move away.

He went along to the front door. Two Scotland Yard men were in the passage and when he reached the foyer two more stood about, and there was another couple as well as a uniformed man outside. One of the plain-clothes men said:

'Everything all right with Mrs. Dawlish, sir?'

'She's taking it very well,' Neil answered. This man, everyone but the few, believed that Mr. Dawlish was dead.

'She would,' the man remarked.

'Do you know her?' Neil asked.

'Everyone who's ever worked for Mr. Dawlish either knows her or knows what she's like, sir. Mr. Dawlish's right arm.'

'Sure,' Neil said. 'Sure, she's great.' He walked towards the corner and a chauffeur moved from the seat of a car; it was the man who had driven him here. He had intended to walk, to get the black mood out of him. He *would* walk.

'Can I take you anywhere, sir?'

'No,' Neil said. 'No thanks, I'll check with Mr. Scott later.'

'Very good, sir.'

Neil began to stride out, towards and past the doors of Westminister Abbey, across the street from the Houses of Parliament. Traffic was thin in Parliament Square and he crossed it easily, and paused, as he always did, to look at the statue of Abraham Lincoln. He became aware of the vast gulf between this home of democracy and the one at Washington; and at the same moment became acutely aware of the equally vast gulf between British people and American. Everything was fine while things went along smoothly between two people or the two peoples, but when one or the other miscued – oh, what the hell! Once he was in Whitehall, dwarfed by buildings which neverthelesss were low and squat compared with many in New York but similar to many in Washington, his anger with himself and the situation began to slacken. It was past time he took a clear detached look at things as they were.

He was here simply as an American delegate to the Crime Haters, and he had no authority. He could think, talk, advise, even act – but he could not give orders or make decisions. On his own he was worse off than he would be when the three men arrived from Rome. Meanwhile: what could he do?

He had been planning to talk to Violetta.

That thought was hardly in his mind than he began to get hot under the collar. Had Felicity any idea what she had done? Violetta might have provided some vital piece of information by now. She might have started the police on a campaign which could have brought the Farenza crashing. *Felicity had been crazy!*

Why?

Simply because she thought she knew better than he? Or was there some reason he didn't begin to suspect? Could she want someone else to crack the problem? Could this conceivably be a patriotic motivation?

'Hold it,' he said aloud. 'Don't you be crazy, Neil Commyns.' He quickened his pace past the Cenotaph and was soon at Trafalgar Square but he hardly looked at the bronze lions and the fountains and the thousands of pigeons swarming about children handing out corn, and turned into the Strand. It would be interesting to see how closely the Celestia shop was watched; how well the Yard was doing its job.

At least he'd been consulted about what to do with Mario Galli, who would be on his way back from the airport by now. He passed Charing Cross Station and a newsvendor who wore a bow tie and a bowler hat. The man held out a *Sunday Times*, and said:

'*A man just went into Celestia Travel, Mr. Commyns.*'

Neil was rocked back on his heels by the remark, by the fact that this must be a C.I.D. man. Now he knew how closely the shop was watched! Next moment he was rocked again. Why would anyone want to get into the travel agency? To collect documents? *Or to destroy them?* On reflex he said: 'We must get him!' He strode towards the shop as a car pulled up alongside him, the door swung open, and Gordon Scott appeared. It was like a conjuring trick. The front door of the shop was closed and there were no lights on inside. Scott nodded to Neil and tried the door, but it was locked. He used a form of picklock with which Neil was unfamiliar, and almost at once the door sprang open and he stepped inside. Two other men appeared, behind Neil; the remarkable thing was their silence.

Scott reached the door leading to a square hallway, with a small automatic lift and a flight of carpeted stairs. He went up the stairs like a streak, and reached the landing above. Only a second behind him, Neil saw the man in an office on the right; he did not know it was Galli's office.

The man had a small box in his hand.

He was short, dark-haired, dark-eyed. He looked appalled at the sight of Neil, and for a split second stood unmoving. In that brief space of time Gordon Scott leapt. The box in the other's hand might be high explosive, might be enough to blow them to little pieces, but Scott hurled himself bodily forward. The short man darted back and threw the box at Scott, who grabbed at it and missed.

It hurtled towards Neil.

He saw it; could have dodged to one side, for cover. Instead, he cupped his hands as he might as a baseball came towards him. He held it. Nothing happened. *He held it.* The little man gave a choking gasp and dashed wildly towards the door. *He's afraid of it*, Neil thought, *he expects it to go off*. He remembered the cloakroom. One of the policemen on the landing dived for the small man and held him as he screamed:

'Fire! Fire!'

Neil held the box in one hand, reached the cloakroom dropped it gently into the water closet, and turned swiftly away. The cry of *'Fire, fire!'* was still echoing. He reached the door and closed it – and as he did so a roar came, the door rocked, there was a rumbling sound and a furious gust of wind and a billowing of red-tinged smoke. One of Scott's men already had a fire extinguisher in his hand and was knocking the nozzle and pointing it towards the door. Neil felt his mouth dry, his lips parched, his body numbed. He swayed. Gordon Scott held him by the shoulders and moved towards the office. Neil went in and half-sat, half-leaned against the big, flat-topped desk. Scott spoke to one of the other men. A red glow appeared at the bottom of the clockroom door, and the landing was thick with acrid-smelling smoke. Other men, shadowy figures to Neil, were at the landing. Scott left them alone. He shivered involuntarily, but began to feel better. He took a pack of Kent from his pocket, struck a match from a book, and drew in the tobacco smoke. In the distance sounded the ringing of alarm bells; the fire engine, of course.

Scott came back, sturdy, smoke-grimed, eyes watering.

'Are you all right?'

'Sure,' Neil said, 'I'm okay.'

'That was a bloody fine thing to do.'

Neil waved both hands, in disclaimer.

'The kind of crazy thing Pat Dawlish would do,' Scott went on.

'Don't try to make me a hero,' Neil said, but he felt a fierce glow of pride. 'Did it work?'

'The door's nearly burnt through,' answered Scott. 'If that bomb had exploded in here nothing would have been saved. As it is we'll be able to search every file in the office, and most of the building will be saved. A fire engine's on the way.' He moved towards the door, still looking at Neil. 'And if it had gone off on the landing, none of us here would be alive. Everyone knows that.'

Neil stubbed out his cigarette.

'I'm very glad,' he said. The comment seemed trite, but there was nothing else he could think of. 'Do you need me here any more?'

'Not unless you want to stay.'

'I ought to clean up for the others from Rome,' said Neil. 'Do you know what time they'll be here? I know you told me, but I've forgotten.'

'Their flight's been delayed,' answered Scott. 'They won't be here until nearly eleven, their plane's due at Heathrow at ten o'clock. They'll stay at your hotel,' Scott went on. 'Why don't you wait there? I'll let you know if anything transpires here or anywhere else.'

'Thanks. That's just what I'll do,' Neil declared.

Firemen were already running hoses up the stairs from two tenders nearby. A big crowd was cordoned off by policemen; the same car and driver were waiting in the Strand for Neil. He leaned back and closed his eyes, still feeling a little lost and shaken, and heavy-hearted. He had no doubt at all that it was because of the way he and Felicity had parted.

In his hospital room in Rome, Dawlish had his most lucid interval yet. And there was a hardness in his voice when he said:

'I want to talk to my wife.'

'You will see her soon,' the surgeon-in-charge assured him. 'Do not worry, Mr. Dawlish. If you will please take this medicine . . .'

'But I do worry,' Dawlish insisted in a weak kind of growl.

He had no choice but to take the pills he was given; soon, no choice but to fall into a drugged sleep.

CHAPTER FOURTEEN

THE COMMITTEE OF FOUR

NEIL COMMYNS slipped out of his clothes when he reached the quiet of his hotel room, which was large and comfortable; one corner was quite luxurious with two armchairs, a television and a coffee-table. He had a shower, put on a lightweight dressing-gown, and sat back in one of the armchairs. He had a throbbing headache, and his eyes burned, probably from the chemical in the bomb. He felt nauseated, too, and did not understand why he should feel so bad; he had endured much more danger and action, at least as much emotional stress in the past ...

'Goddammit!' he exclaimed aloud, 'I'm plain hungry!'

He reached for the telephone, ordered an omelette with ham and some coffee and toast, then sat back, still wryly amused with himself but sharply aware of the eggs and bacon which Felicity had cooked. Why the hell had she put Violetta to sleep? And why the hell had he lost his temper? That was a thing he took great pride in: he never lost his temper.

It was a little after six o'clock when he finished the meal. Already he felt much better and on edge to know what, if anything, had been found at the shop in the Strand. Gordon Scott would call if there were developments of importance; Scott, in action, was quite a guy. All of the police he had met here were good, and he derived from them all a feeling of integrity; of doing whatever they did out of a sense of vocation.

Was that crazy thinking?

The word 'crazy' came too often and too easily to his mind today.

He sat back and closed his eyes, and was actually half-asleep when the telephone bell rang, not even sure what it was. Realizing it, he grabbed, thinking: This will be Scott.

'Neil Commyns,' he said.

'Neil.' It was Felicity Dawlish, and his heart leapt. Now he had no doubt at all how much she had been in his heart and on his mind. 'Are you all right?' When he didn't answer at first, being taken off his balance, she went on: 'I've heard about the fire in the Strand.'

'Oh,' he said. 'News certainly gets around.'

'*Are* you all right?' she demanded.

He paused again; he thought Felicity drew in a deep breath, as if she felt rebuffed; and then he went on, more relaxed than he had been for hours:

'Yes, I'm fine. I feel the worst kind of heel where you're concerned, Felicity, but I can still get mad at you. Does that make any sense?'

With a funny kind of laughing voice, Felicity answered: 'It's exactly how I feel about you!'

'It must mean something.' Neil felt a glow of relief spread through him, making not only his body but his arms and legs, even his fingers and toes, tingle with unfamiliar warmth.

'You really weren't hurt in the fire?' she persisted.

'I wasn't even scratched.'

'If you'd been unlucky you could have been burned to death.'

'Maybe,' he conceded. 'And maybe I was born lucky.' He paused for a fraction of a moment before going on: 'If I'm allowed to ask, how is Violetta?'

'She's still asleep, but her pulse is much stronger,' Felicity told him. It was her turn to pause, and Neil made himself wait. The sense of warmth remained but the tingling had gone; it was as if a heavy burden had been lifted from his chest. Then in a different voice, a tone he hadn't heard before, Felicity went on: 'Will you promise not to laugh at me?'

'I won't laugh,' he assured her.

'I have such a strange feeling.'

'What kind of feeling?'

There was another pause. It conveyed her sense of anxiety, perhaps of apprehension. He had the feeling that she had reached the crux of her reason for telephoning. He had a different thought: that she was finding it difficult to say what she wanted to say; perhaps it was because he could hear her breathing in a way which was almost a series of gasps.

'Neil,' she said at last, 'I think Pat is trying to – to get through to me.'

He did not speak, but thought with a clutch of fear at his heart: Does she mean she thinks he's dead?

'I've felt the same kind of thing before,' she went on.

'With reason?' he asked, and added quickly, afraid the words could be misunderstood: 'I mean, with justification afterwards?'

'Sometimes, yes.'

'Sixth sense?' He kept his voice level; rational.

'Or presentiment,' she replied. 'Pat always laughed and called it' – she caught her breath, but Neil didn't interrupt, and she finished – 'a hunch.'

'He works on hunches, doesn't he?' As he said that all that he had been told about Dawlish poured through his mind: things which Randy Patton of the New York Police had told him, and the two men were close friends. Things which other officers had told him, even Salvatori and Pierre-Jacques. Dawlish undoubtedly had some quality which none of them really understood. Dawlish himself pooh-poohed it, declaring that he knew the facts and assessed them, made the obvious deductions and acted accordingly. But Randy Patton was a hard-headed, cynical policeman with over twenty years' experience in one of the toughest police forces in the world.

'Do you know what he's trying to say?' Neil asked.

'No. Oh no! I just feel he . . .' She caught her breath again. 'I keep hearing his voice in my mind.'

'Felicity,' Neil said, his tone a mixutre of gentleness and firmness, 'are you trying to tell me that you think he's in danger?'

'No,' she responded at once. 'I don't get that feeling at all.'

'Then what?'

'That he's trying to tell me *I'm* in danger,' she replied.

'Ah,' exclaimed Neil. 'That makes good sense. Are the Yard men still outside the door?'

'Oh yes,' she assured him. 'And two are in the flat.'

'Keep them there.'

'I will!' There was no doubt how seriously she took the 'hunch'. 'Neil, could you make sure that everything's all right in Rome?'

'So you *do* think he's in danger?' Now his voice was sharper because of his own fear.

It was some time before she answered. He could hear her breathing but it was not laboured now; in fact it was very even, her mouth must be close to the mouth-piece. He wished he were with her so that he could see her expression and draw conclusions from it.

'Neil,' she said at last.

'Yes.'

'That wasn't like you.'

'I don't understand.'

'Of course he's in danger,' she said. 'He always is.'

There was a sudden flood of anguish through him. For the first time he really understood how she felt; knew that whenever Dawlish was away on an investigation, she lived with fear which she managed to bury deep within herself. And she was right. Moreover, he hadn't given a thought to the possibility that Dawlish might be in danger from more than the consequences of the operation. That, cunningly though the pretence had been carried out and closely though the secret had been kept, the Farenza might know he was alive and make another attempt to kill him.

These thoughts flashed through his mind so quickly that there was hardly a pause between Felicity's comment and his response.

'In times of crisis all of us are in danger. Felicity, are you sure you're not simply suffering from a kind of reaction? That the presentiment isn't born of fear?'

'No, I'm not sure,' she admitted. 'Pat often explained it away like that.'

After a moment he went on: 'Is there anything specific you want me to do?'

'I wish you could be in Rome,' she told him.

'I'd be no use there, I don't speak Italian, but . . .'

She was suddenly excited; hopeful. 'You've thought of something!'

'I've friends in Rome,' he said, briskly. 'Two F.B.I. men who . . .' He broke off.

'Go on!' she urged.

'But I'm not sure I ought to let them into the secret. And

even if I did I wouldn't be able to tell them where Pat is. Honey, let me think about it.'

'Yes, of course,' Felicity said, an edge of disappointment in her voice.

He felt momentary exasperation. In these circumstances why on earth should she feel disappointed? Then he reminded himself that she must be living on her nerves, that much of her life she had been going from crisis to crisis. In the background he heard a voice, another voice. Both were men's, both would be Yard officers.

'I'll call you back,' he promised, and rang off.

He was exasperated in turn with himself, for fear he had shown his impatience. He stood up, with his hand on the telephone. The contentment he had felt when he had made peace with Felicity had gone, in its place was a mood of tension and uncertainty. Things were wrong. He had missed out somewhere, and did not yet understand why. Why *should* Felicity feel disappointed after what he had said? She couldn't have expected him to work miracles.

What had he said?

'But I'm not sure I ought to let them into the secret. And even if I did I wouldn't be able to tell them where Pat is.'

There was the cause of disappointment: he didn't know where Pat was. If she had thought he could get someone in Rome to go and see him, to check on the safety measures, she would naturally be acutely disappointed when she realized he couldn't do even such a simple thing.

Why couldn't he?

Why didn't he know where Dawlish was?

Because he had never been told and had made no attempt to inquire. He had simply taken the word of Salvatori and Pierre-Jacques that Dawlish was somewhere safe and being well guarded.

Two possibilities arose out of this, each giving him a sickening sense of uselessness. The precautions to protect Dawlish might not be good enough; that was an occupational hazard, whatever defences one put up there was always a way to circumvent it. Or: *Salvatori or Pierre-Jacques might not be trustworthy.* The possibility struck him as if he had been poleaxed.

'It's a crazy idea!' he blurted out aloud.

'Crazy' again. But was it, in fact?

Salvatori was an Italian from an old family, and many of the Farenza came from the oldest families in Italy.

It was ludicrous!

If Salvatori or Pierre-Jacques was involved no one in the Farenza would have been fooled for a moment about Dawlish's 'death', but – *had* they really been fooled? What were the indications? The arrangements by the Farenza here had been made very quickly – almost as if they had known there was a crisis. He, Neil Commyns, was new to the Crime Haters, to the individuals as well as to their methods. He had been pitched into the situation with too little knowledge and experience. Whom could he trust absolutely? He had to remind himself that he was almost certainly wrong about Salvatori and Pierre-Jacques, but now that the suspicion was rooted in his mind he would never be able to rest until he could be absolutely assured.

'I must talk to Randy,' he said aloud.

What time was it in New York? he asked himself. Six hours earlier than here. What did it matter? If he had to get Randy out of bed, okay, he would get Randy out of bed. He gave a fierce smile and stretched down for the telephone: and *froze.*

Something clicked in his mind: like a shutter opening.

The last time he had been on the telephone, five minutes ago, he had heard two men's voices somewhere behind Felicity. Scotland Yard officers, he had remarked to himself, and now suddenly he realized that they might not have been.

One of them had spoken with a European accent.

In Chicago, in New York, almost anywhere in the United States, that would have been normal enough, and nothing to notice beyond the simple fact. But this was London, England. English policemen did not speak with European accents. Someone other than Yard men had been in Felicity Dawlish's flat, and he had lost precious time doing nothing. Felicity – *and* Violetta – might be in acute danger. In the process of thinking he dialled Whitehall 1212, still Dawlish's number. It seemed a long time before there was an answer. He gritted his teeth and clenched his hands.

Suddenly a woman operator said: 'Deputy Assistant Commissioner's office.'

'Mr. Gordon Scott, Deputy A.C., please – urgently.'

'Hold on.'

He held on. The seconds ticked by. He felt a restrained fury because he did not know what had happened or for how long he must wait. For a second time an answer came at the moment when he felt like hurling the instrument at the wall. 'Gordon Scott here.'

Neil said: 'This is Neil Commyns.'

'Oh, hallo, sir! I was just going to call you.'

'Is everything all right at Dawlish's flat?' Neil demanded.

'As far as I know, yes,' Scott said. And sharply: 'Have you any reason to think anything's wrong?'

'Nearly ten minutes ago when talking to her, I heard a voice in the background. I've only just realized the man had a European accent. Would one of your men . . .?'

Scott broke in, harshly: 'No, it wouldn't be one of my men. I'll check by radio.' The pause which followed lasted only a moment. 'If someone's got in there we've got to be hellish careful. Where are you now?'

'My hotel.'

'I'll meet you outside the south doors of Westminster Abbey,' Scott said, and rang off.

Very slowly, and with great deliberation, Neil replaced the receiver. He knew that the rendezvous was within two minutes' walk of Dawlish's flat; that Scott had selected it because it was out of sight of anyone in the penthouse; and believed that Scott was as sure as he that the women in the flat were in acute danger.

He had a flash thought: Of the awful irony there would be if Dawlish lived and Felicity died.

CHAPTER FIFTEEN

THE MENACE

FELICITY was vaguely aware that two men were speaking as Neil Commyns put down his receiver. She had felt sick with disappointment at learning that Neil did not know where Pat was; a futile kind of disappointment because she did not know for certain that her fears were justified. Then, without giving her time to think, one of the men spoke in an unfamiliar voice.

She could have called out to Neil: 'Hold on!' Instead, with a reflex action, she put down the receiver and stared over her shoulder at the man in the doorway who levelled a gun at her. She was shocked into disbelief. Two of Gordon Scott's men were here. She had seen them, and one had often worked for Pat, yet – *this* man wasn't one of them. He was short and black-haired and bright-eyed. An Italian or a Spaniard, the cut of his suit was Italian, too. The gun was steady in his hand. She remembered what he had said:

'There is no danger now.'

He had been speaking to someone else, of course; the police had not been able to stop them.

Now he advanced into the room slowly, watching her as he said: 'You needa not worry, please.' She made an involuntary movement back to the telephone, and he said waspishly:

'Keep away from da telephono.'

She actually touched it, but as she did so he moved with bewildering speed, gripped her wrist and pulled her away. She went staggering, caught her leg against the couch, and pitched on to it.

'You maka no noise.' He stood over her, the gun only a foot away from her face.

She struggled up to a sitting position, and straightened her skirt. The man watched her, but she had a sense that he was listening intently for sounds from the passage. There were

Yard men inside and outside, remember. She didn't speak, but breathed heavily through her mouth; the sudden attack had put her out of breath.

The gun in the man's pale hand did not shake.

What did he expect to hear?

Another man appeared in the doorway leading from the hall. He was taller, thinner, red-haired, with the curiously milky-looking skin some southern Europeans have. He wore a close-fitting rust-coloured suit of smooth-textured material. He was smiling. He came in and closed the door, looking at Felicity all the time. She thought almost in desperation: *How did they get in?*

He also spoke in English with a marked áccent.

'It is alla right.'

'You are sure?' demanded the man by Felicity's side.

'Those outside heard nothing. The two inside, they are dead.'

Felicity thought, sickeningly: *Dead*.

The man's eyes were honey-coloured; tawny. They looked strange. He had sharp, rather raw-looking features, as if his face had never been quite finished. There was a quality of evil in him; Felicity had met that too often to have any doubts. He came further into the room, looking at her as he spoke to the dark-haired man, who had moved away from her and who had slipped his gun into his pocket. The other did not show any weapon, either.

The red-haired man said to her: 'Where is Violetta Casselli?'

There was no point in refusing to answer, for they would find the girl in a few seconds; so Felicity moistened her lips, and said:

'In the spare bedroom.'

'Bedroom?'

'Yes,' she said.

'Sleeping?'

'Yes.'

Flame seemed to flare up in the man's eyes.

'She is not dead!'

'No,' Felicity said, wearily. 'She is not dead.' She thought: Not yet.

There was a short pause before the red-haired man ordered: 'Watch her. Do not let her move.' He went back to the doorway, and out into the hallway. He made no sound, and the only sound Felicity could hear was her own breathing. She was very tense. It would be better to relax, but she could not. She watched the door. If there was any cause for relief, it was the man's harsh *'She is not dead!'* So, presumably, Violetta was in no immediate danger. She would be unconscious for at least another hour, perhaps two. Two hours, locked up here with these men!

The red-haired man returned.

His hair *was* red: a peculiar shade which looked as if it were artificial; yet his eyebrows and eyelashes were of the same shade, a flat, opaque, gingery red. His lips were moist. He closed the door behind him with great care, then moved towards her. His movements were slow, he reminded her of a great ginger cat. He stood looking down on her, crowding her so that to try to get away from him she had to press further and harder against the couch.

He put his left hand inside his tight-fitting, beautifully tailored suit, and drew it out, slowly.

Now he held a knife; or dagger.

It was a dagger, with a tapering blade and what looked like a gold hilt. He held it lightly; loosely. She could not look away from it and she could not fail to see the streaks of blood on the blade. It had ben carelessly wiped. There was fresh blood on his hand, too. He held the dagger between his thumb and fingers, only a foot away from her face.

He said: 'I could cutta your throat.'

She gulped.

'Like I cutta da throats of the two men who were here to protect you,' he went on.

The words 'protect you' sounded like a sneer, underlining the fact that no one could protect her now. *How had they got in?* What were the Yard men on the landing doing; were they dead, too?

She closed her eyes to shut out the streaks of brown on the shimmering blade. For a moment there was utter silence, and then she jumped at a sharp pain on her neck, unable to hide the fact that she was desperately afraid.

He held the point of the dagger to her throat. He was smiling. He had very fine, even teeth, and his lips had that raw look.

'I could cutta your throat,' he repeated. 'And if you do not answer my question, I shall cut slow.'

He would, she sensed, whether she answered or not.

She could feel warmth where the point of the dagger had broken the skin, but she did not put her hand to her neck, simply stared up at the man. She must control her fears. The shock had been so great that all her defences had collapsed, but she felt better now; she must not let him think that by a word or by a movement of the dagger he could terrify her.

She managed to say in a hoarse voice: 'What questions?'

'Your husband,' he said. 'Is he dead?'

She thought desperately: Will it do any harm, now, if I tell the truth? Isn't the damage done? Hadn't Neil Commyns and the others used the deception as much as it could be of true value? Hadn't the explosion at the shop in the Strand shown the Farenza that the police knew a great deal, and would they not think that Pat had talked?

The knife nicked her skin.

She was desperately afraid for her own life, yet made herself think. The deception over Pat must have been to deceive the Farenza and make them doubt how much the police knew; but now it was open war. She had to make a decision *now*.

'Is he dead?' the man insisted.

The knife scratched beneath the chin. She felt as sure as she could be that he would kill her, and she did not think the secret was worth dying for.

She said: 'No.'

'*You admit that?*' the other almost cried.

'They thought he was dead but he did not die,' she told him. Her voice was hoarse, and doubts began to crowd in lest she had done irreparable harm, she might have fooled herself by wishful thinking into believing that secrecy no longer mattered.

'Who told you this?' the red-haired man demanded.

'Neil – Neil Commyns.'

'So.' The other breathed heavily, as if with satisfaction. 'Whose body they bury instead of your husband body?'

'I don't know,' she replied.

He looked at her as if trying to make up his mind whether to believe her or not. He toyed with the dagger, and then put it slowly away. Relief oozed through her veins like a physical thing. The other man stood a few feet away, watching disinterestedly. The red-haired man spoke to him in Italian and he moved to the window which was flush with the wall of the high building, and peered down; she knew he was looking into the street, and the carriageway below, doubtless to see if there was any unusual police activity. Presumably there was not, for the man came back, spreading his hand.

'All is okay,' he said.

'*Bruno.*' The red-haired man turned back to Felicity. 'What did Violetta tell you?'

'Nothing,' she answered quickly.

'You must not lie to me.'

'She wasn't able to tell me anything,' Felicity said, and when the other nodded, ordering her to continue, she went on: 'Neil Commyns brought her here. He wanted to ask her questions, but I – I drugged her.'

'*You* drugga her?'

'She needed rest.'

'But you are the wife of Dawlish.'

'I am a woman,' Felicity said.

She wondered where this was going to get her, how it could possibly end. And: *How had these men got into the penthouse?* There was silence for a few moments as if the man was turning question and answer over in his mind. The silence was broken by the sound of an aeroplane engine, very close to the roof. She was aware of it but took no notice as she watched the red-haired man's face. The word 'evil' came back to her: raw evil.

At last he said in the most casual voice: 'There will not be mucha woman left of you if you lie to me.'

Her breath hissed in: 'I am not lying.'

'What did Violetta say to this Commyns?'

'I don't think she said anything.'

'He was here a long time – he would have told you.'

'No,' Felicity denied. 'He is a secretive man.'

'What do you mean by that?'

'He trusts no one,' she said.

'And he did not question Violetta?'

'I don't think he did.'

'Are you not sure?'

'I am nearly sure,' Felicity said, very quickly. 'He was very angry when I put her to sleep.'

'Angry?' the man shouted. 'Why?'

'Because he wanted to talk to her.' When those strangely smouldering eyes asked their questions she went on: 'If she had spoken to him he would not have had reason to be so angry.'

'So!' the red-haired man exclaimed as if with satisfaction. 'She has not talked.' He threw back his head and laughed deep in his throat, a horrible sound because it told her how deeply pleased he was, and he could only show such pleasure if she had told him everything he had wanted to know. 'Benito', he said to the other man.

'What is it?' Benito asked.

'We need not trouble to take Violetta away,' the red-haired man declared. 'We do not have to find out what she said to this Commyns, because she said nothing. So she will never be able to tell them.'

Felicity felt claws at her heart as she thought: Oh dear God, what have I done?

The other was saying: 'We have only to kill her and to escape ourselves.'

The dark-haired man said eagerly: '*Si, si!*'

He stared at Felicity.

The red-haired man was also looking at her and with even greater intentness. She sat still as a statue, wondering despairingly what she could do to save the girl. She knew why these men were staring, knew what was in their minds. They would kill her also. But somehow that did not seem to matter. She had been dreadfully wrong to put Violetta to sleep; she had been terribly guilty of a kind of treachery when she had convinced these men that Violetta had not talked. She had thought it was a good thing, that it would save the Italian girl. Instead it was her death warrant.

Was there nothing she could do?

If she threw herself at the red-haired man with his hateful expression – oh, nonsense! He would stick that dagger into her or cut her throat. Nothing she could do would save Violetta. Everything she had done had been harmful. Deadly.

The hopelessness must have shown on her face.

A glint, which might be just the lust to kill, sparked in the red-haired man's eyes. She saw his lips turn back and she knew he was going to draw out the dagger. She tried not to watch his hand but could not prevent herself. It was like waiting for death.

Across the awful silence the telephone bell jarred.

It made the red-haired man jump. It made the other spin round. It made her turn her head. The telephone was on a table at the end of the couch. *Burr-burr* it rang: *burr-burr*. Abruptly, the red-haired man moved. He grabbed her wrist and pulled her up and thrust her towards the telephone. He spoke in Italian to the other man who sprang towards the kitchen – obviously for the extension.

'*Answer!*' hissed the red-haired man. '*Answer!*'

She almost fell, steadied, and lifted the telephone. She was gasping for breath, a noise which would surely sound over the microphone. The man let her wrist go, and slapped her across the face.

'*Answer!*'

She drew a deep breath, and managed to sound quite calm.

'This is Felicity Dawlish.'

'Good evening, Mrs. Dawlish.' The speaker had a pleasant, English voice, and a curiously confiding tone. 'I wonder if you can help me.' Before she could speak, he went on: 'And please do forgive me for this intrusion at such a time. My name is Regan, of the *Daily Record*. Denis Regan.'

'What – what is it you want?' Felicity asked. The man at the other end of the line must surely know there was something the matter, her voice was so strange, and she gasped between each word.

'Mrs. Dawlish, I have been told that Mr. Dawlish visited a travel agency in the Strand just before leaving for Rome and that tragic happening. I *do* apologize for worrying you now, but was Mr. Dawlish investigating the affairs of the travel agency – the Celestia Agency? And is that why he went to Rome?'

She caught her breath.

The red-haired man was now in front of her, dagger in hand.

'I – I don't know,' she managed to say. 'My husband didn't discuss his official business with me. 'Good – good-bye.'

'Mrs. Dawlish!' the caller cried as if in alarm. 'I know it's an unforgiveable intrusion, but . . .'

Somewhere in the flat there was a sound: a soft *zutt*! of sound. A tiny bright shape appeared close to the telephone and burst. A cloud of vapour billowed up and suddenly fumes bit at her eyes and nose and mouth. She dropped the telephone and staggered to one side; she saw the red-haired man staggering, and also saw the dagger glinting as it fell from his hand. She heard his harsh breathing. The pain at her eyes and mouth was awful, she felt as if she was going to die of suffocation.

A man appeared out of nowhere and supported her.

Soon she was in the bathroom.

The man wrapped a towel round her shoulders and began to bathe her face. The pain eased. She could hear voices. She knew that she was safe. She still could not see because tears of pain blurred her vision, but she could recognize the voice of the man who was bathing her eyes and lips with such gentleness as he kept on saying:

'It's all right, honey. It's all right. Don't worry, honey, everything's all right.'

It was Neil Commyns.

CHAPTER SIXTEEN

ARRIVALS FROM ROME

FELICITY felt much better. Her eyes still felt tender and her lips and throat sore, but she could see clearly, for the tears had dried up and the biting pain had subsided. Now she was in the kitchen, and Neil was pouring milk into a glass. He had left the

refrigerator door open and she kept thinking: He ought close it. Pat was always leaving it open.

He put the bottle on the working surface, closed the refrigerator door with his knee, and held the milk towards her.

'It will do you good,' he assured her.

She didn't usually like milk ice-cold from the refrigerator, but this was lovely, soothing, cooling, invigorating. She sipped cautiously at first, then gulped greedily until the glass was empty. By that time Gordon Scott had arrived in the kitchen; he looked a little red about the eyes too. It was surprisingly cold in here – goodness, the windows were wide open!

'Better?' asked Neil.

'Much!'

'If there's plenty of milk, I wouldn't mind a glass,' Gordon Scott put in.

'There's plenty,' Neil told him.

Felicity found herself saying: 'Of course, you know.'

'I have eyes,' Neil opened the door again.

'Help yourself,' Felicity said. She could hardly stop a giggle. 'Will someone please tell me what happened?'

Scott drank half the milk at one gulp, lowered the glass, and smiled from her to Neil.

'Guardian angel Commyns realized that a Yard man wouldn't be likely to speak with a European accent,' he said. 'So we knew something was badly wrong. One of our men pretended to be a newspaperman, and telephoned to distract the attention of the chaps here. Then we unlocked the door – there was a key at the office – and used tear-gas pistols to put them out of action immediately, without injuring them so that they can't talk.'

'How on earth did they get *in*?' demanded Felicity.

'From the roof,' Gordon told her simply. 'There is a fire gangway which can be stretched across between this building and the next, and they simply climbed across. Then they were close to the penthouse, and came in through a window. If either of them had slipped on the gangway he would have broken his neck.' Gordon Scott finished the milk, and put the glass down on the bar. 'Thank you, that was good,' he said. He wiped the sweat off his forehead, and went on very slowly: 'Man after man risks his life without hesitation, for the Farenza. And they

kill without compunction. The two Yard men on duty in your hallway were killed. The men on the landing had no idea what was going on.'

Felicity said: 'They told me they'd killed them.' She had a mental picture of the dagger, and shuddered. 'Do you – do you think we're anywhere near the end?'

'Nearer, for certain,' Neil said reassuringly.

'How can we be sure?'

'They wouldn't have taken such risks to get at Violetta if she didn't know something of vital importance,' Neil answered.

That was so obviously true that the question had hardly been necessary. She wasn't at all herself. If the truth were told, she hadn't been since she had first heard of Pat's 'death'. She had felt normal enough but had always been on the edge of the abnormal; such as when she had given Violetta the sleeping pills. She had a feeling that Neil wasn't really himself, either. There was so little breathing space, the pressure built up all the time.

'Neil,' she said, 'don't you really know where Pat is?'

Gordon Scott looked from one to the other, as if asking silently: Hey! What's all this?

Neil said: 'No. He was at the Santa Maria Hospital at first and moved from there. Salvatori didn't tell me on the agreement that the fewer people who knew, the safer Pat was.' He looked at Scott. 'Did you know?'

Scott was looking very young yet very tense.

'No,' he answered. 'You mean – he's not dead?' Slowly, Commyns shook his head, and Scott cried: 'Then why the devil . . .?'

He broke off. The silence was almost frightening, and it was a sharp anticlimax when one of the Yard men came in. He was stocky, grey-haired, sombre-looking.

'Excuse me, sir.'

'Yes, Webster?' Scott said.

'The prisoners are ready to be moved.'

'Take them to Cannon Row,' Scott ordered, and added with grim emphasis: 'Is the convoy ready?'

'Two cars ahead and two behind, and a bullet-proof van for the prisoners.'

'Good,' Scott said, and when Webster didn't go, he asked: 'What else?'

'You realize there are two prisoners at Cannon Row already, don't you, sir?'

'Yes. What about it?'

The other drew in his breath.

'It would be better to keep them apart, would it, sir?'

Scott looked puzzled, but that was more pretence than fact; he wanted to know exactly what was in the other man's mind. Felicity knew this old and experienced Yard man was afraid there might be an attack on the police station; the Farenza had worried him as much as that. Neil Commyns must know that, too.

'Why keep them apart?' Scott asked.

'Just a precaution, sir.'

'I'll check,' Scott promised. 'Lodge them at Cannon Row for the time being.'

'Right, sir. I – oh! I forgot these photographs. They've just arrived by messenger.' He handed Scott the large envelope and went out, obviously far from satisfied about Cannon Row. Scott opened the envelope slowly, giving the impression that he was not thinking about what he was doing. Felicity had a strange idea; that she would like to scream. There was something in the situation which created hysteria. Then Commyns said very quietly: 'He was very near death, and we thought there was no hope. But he survived and I came to tell Felicity.'

Scott gulped, then muttered: 'Thank God.' He gulped again, then made himself take out the photographs. Felicity saw them and her thoughts changed with relief.

'Gordon! That's the man at the pub in the Lake District.' She was excited as she picked up the photograph of a dark-haired man. 'The man who was there when I went in about my car.'

'I know who you mean,' Gordon Scott said. 'He was caught outside with a car, waiting for the two who tried to kill Violetta this afternoon. When you come to think of it,' he went on, 'they really want to make sure Violetta can't talk, don't they, sir?' Looking at Neil, he was obviously weighing a question up in his mind. He voiced it at last, as if it troubled him very much.

'Will you question her at once, or will you wait until the others arrive from Rome?'

Neil did not hesitate.

'As soon as she comes round,' he declared.

Gordon Scott nodded his agreement. There was no time to wait for anyone, least of all men who, though leaders of the police in their native land, had become suspect. That might be absurd, might prove to be wholly unjust, but the question had arisen.

'I wish . . .' Neil began, but broke off.

'What do you wish?' Scott asked.

'I wish we knew where Dawlish was.' Now he glanced at Felicity.

'We shall as soon as the others arrive,' Scott said. Then harshly: 'If Salvatori doesn't tell us . . .' He broke off.

'Well?' Neil asked roughly.

'We'll have to find out why,' Scott growled, and then he bunched a fist and thumped it into the palm of his other hand. 'Oh, to hell with it! We need Pat Dawlish, that's who we need here.' He thumped his palm again. 'It just doesn't make sense to suspect men like Salvatori, Pierre-Jacques and Lohn, yet for some reason I do. I wish to God . . .' He broke off, looking a little shame-facedly at the others.

An aeroplane droned overhead.

Only a hundred miles or so away, flying over the English Channel off the Normandy coast, was the *Al Italia* Boeing 707 which was bringing the other three members of the governing committee of the Crime Haters. The plane was nearly full. The journey had been uneventful, and gave promise of staying that way. The evening was very clear and the stars shone vividly.

Far behind the aircraft, in Rome, Dawlish was in a drugged coma.

Ahead of the aircraft, in London, Violetta Casselli was stirring out of her drugged sleep. She looked too young and too beautiful to know any vital secrets of the Farenza.

The three police chiefs read or dozed or actually slept in the first-class cabin. They had talked themselves dry, and had come to the common conclusion that there was now nothing they could do until they could talk to Neil Commyns, Gordon Scott and, perhaps, Felicity.

Two or three passengers pushed their faces against the small windows, seeing the English coastline, unmistakable in the moonlight. Even the white froth of the waves as they broke on the beaches showed up clearly. The stillness below seemed absolute, apart from the breakers. The lights of a village seemed to be those of another world. The only sound was the drone of the four jet engines.

Suddenly, awfully, the quiet was ripped by a roar from beneath the floor of the aircraft.

First there was the roar, deafening and terrifying.

Next there were the flames, white hot and horrifying.

Then there was the inrush of air and a screeching and a sound like the wailing of all the hundred and seven human beings on board.

Finally there was a ball of fire in the sky; an inferno; and where there had been the great engines, that aircraft, the crew and the passengers, the little self-contained world, there was nothing.

Only a void.

The R.A.F. aircraft was flying five thousand feet above the *Al Italia* 707. The radio officer, watching the lights as they went on and off, saw the flames from the great ball of fire. Next he saw the ball break into dozens of large pieces of falling debris, like meteorites; and in turn these broke and fell towards the waiting earth; and the first blazing mass of wreckage had struck the earth and burst in meadowland as the radio officer began to report to London Airport and the first alarm began to spread.

On the cliffs there were many young lovers.

Inland, in the copses and the glens and the secret places, were many others.

Some, intent on each other, enraptured, lit by passion, neither heard nor saw the awful thing that happened in the sky. Some girls, staring upwards, passive but compliant, saw the ball of fire and the other fires which fell from it, and cried out and spoiled ecstasy, fear mirrored in their eyes. Others, coupling done or not yet begun, lay side by side and saw first the flash and then the ball of fire and next the showering as of giant fireworks. A few, close by, heard the screech as the main bulk of the aircraft fell, then heard it crash, and saw more flames. A barn caught fire and lit up the countryside for many miles around. No one was hurt on land, not even cattle died; only the hundred and seven human beings who had been alone in their remote world a few minutes before, and now were dead.

In Felicity's apartment the telephone bell rang.

In the spare bedroom Felicity was with Violetta, who was now awake; a little dazed, but wide awake. She was sitting up, with an angora wool jacket about her shoulders, a pale green colour which added prettiness and softness to beauty. Her eyes were rested.

'And you will talk to them,' Felicity urged.

'Yes,' Violetta promised. 'I will tell them all I know. But . . .' She broke off, as Felicity stood up from the side of the bed and the telephone bell rang harshly. There was no extension in here but a direct line to the exchange. Felicity heard Gordon Scott's voice after the ringing stopped. There was a pause, then with stark clarity:

'*My God!*'

Felicity caught her breath. Violetta put down her nearly empty cup of coffee. Felicity moved towards the door. The doors to all the rooms were open and sound travelled clearly.

'Oh, *God!*' breathed Scott again.

Felicity heard another sound: Neil Commyns picking up the extension receiver in the kitchen. She was torn between the desire to go and join the men, and not to desert this girl.

'*All* dead?' Scott's voice was anguished.

All of whom? Not Pat, please God, not Pat!

'Where – where did it happen?' He waited, listening, and after a while went on: 'Yes. Yes, I know . . . In Rome, presumably. Did it stop anywhere?'

There was silence until he said: 'Then the bomb must have been put on board in Rome.' He hesitated, before slowly putting down the receiver. Violetta sat up in bed, her eyes rounded and huge. Felicity stepped into the passage, as the two telephones went down simultaneously, and Gordon Scott said in a flat voice: 'There was a bomb on board the aircraft. A hundred and seven people died, including Salvatori, Pierre-Jacques and Lohn.'

Felicity felt as if her blood had turned to ice, almost as badly as when she had believed that Pat was dead.

Scott went on hoarsely: 'So much for suspecting *them*.'

Neil didn't speak, and it was some time – a long time – before Scott spoke again:

'A hundred and seven lives. They won't stop at a thing.'

'What can be so important?' Felicity found herself asking.

Neil said: 'That is what we are going to find out from Violetta.'

He appeared in the passage from the big room door, Gordon came in from the kitchen, and Felicity half-turned. Neil's face, set and stern, was suddenly full of consternation, and Scott cried out:

'*Stop her!*'

But on his words the door slammed, and only Violetta could have slammed it. Neil passed Felicity like a bullet and flung himself against the door, but a fraction of a second before he thudded into it there was a tiny metallic sound; of the key being turned in the lock. Scott hurtled past Felicity and the two men flung themselves at the door, but it didn't budge.

'She'll kill herself,' Scott rasped. 'We've got to stop her.' He swung round and pushed past Neil and rushed into the adjoining room, which had a window close to the one in the room where Violetta was locked in.

CHAPTER SEVENTEEN

'DON'T JUMP'

NEIL went after Scott, but as the younger man turned into the room, Felicity called out: 'Kitchen, kitchen!' Neil stopped in the middle of a step, turned on one foot, and came towards her. She was already running into the kitchen. The sink and working surfaces were in front of the window, which was in three sections, two of them opening on hinges, the middle one permanently closed. Felicity pushed open the window on the right, and stood aside. As if this had all been rehearsed, Neil climbed up on the working top. Knives and forks, cups and saucers and plates fell into the sink. He sat down, sideways to the window, which was just wide enough for him to squeeze through.

(Scott, much stockier and thickset, would never have got through.)

Neil hitched himself sideways.

Felicity hauled herself up on the other side of the sink, so as to see.

First, there were Neil's head and shoulders. Absurdly, in that moment she noticed that he had the beginning of a bald spot in his hair. Beyond, was Violetta, half-way through her window, staring towards Neil. Below was the great well of the building, twenty storeys or more down, and a paved courtyard below. Staring up from the courtyard were two men, faces and bodies distorted.

'Violetta,' Neil called quietly. 'Don't jump.'

Quiet though they were, the words echoed in the well.

'Doooaaant juuump.'

Violetta did not answer, but hung by her skirt which was caught on the window fastener; this also was a window which opened outward, on hinges.

'Don't jump,' Neil repeated. There was a note of command in his voice; he spoke as Pat would have spoken in the same emergency, trying to quell panic, making the situation seem almost normal. 'They're not worth it.'

He was much further out of the window now.

The wall, of concrete blocks, was built with a series of ledges running right round, above each window. There, pigeons would roost, and shrill-voiced starlings and sparrows. One slip would mean a fall to death.

Violetta was tugging at her skirt, holding on to the window by one hand so as to exert more strength.

Neil was groping with his left leg for the ledge but couldn't reach it. He looked down, and obviously tried to judge the distance. Immediately he drew his leg up and twisted his body so that he was outside in the well, crouching, groping on the ledge outside the window, hands gripping the frame of the window itself.

He's going to lower himself, Felicity thought, in anguish.

Violetta was half out of the bedroom window: tugging, tugging. Her back was towards Neil and Felicity. Her dark hair had fallen to one side, dropping to her shoulders, the other still neatly coiled in.

'Violetta,' Neil called, 'it won't do any good to kill yourself. We shall find the truth with or without your help.'

There was a pause. He was now upright with a toe-hold on the ledge he had been trying to reach, a finger-hold on the ledge outside the kitchen window. So he was below her and below Violetta.

Felicity almost sobbed: What good can you do? You can't save her.

At best, she knew, he could hold on; and only by holding on could he save himself from a fatal fall.

Gordon Scott had disappeared.

'Violetta,' Neil called, 'You are too beautiful to die.'

Did she stop tugging? *Did* she stop trying to free herself? Whether or no, Neil edged towards her on fingers and toes and was soon half-way towards the girl. She was still crouching, and another big lock of hair fell forward, hiding the shape of her head. Suddenly the skirt seemed to unwind, all her long legs showed and only the skirt itself was caught in the window. She had unfastened the waistband, and it was a wrap-over skirt. She could fall now. Yet she was still holding on. Her blouse billowed. She wore white panties and flesh tights on shapely legs.

Neil was within an arm's reach of her, but if he let go he would fall.

'Violetta,' he said calmly, 'it will be such a waste if you kill yourself. No one else will suffer if you live.'

'*If you liiiive,*' the echo came sighing, '*if you liiiive.*'

'We know everything now,' Neil went on. 'Everything that matters.'

'*That matters, that matters, that matters.*'

Violetta still held on with her hands.

Yet she could fall so easily, quickly; had only to release her hold and she would fall to inevitable death. Neil was just a foot or two away from her. His voice was much lower; pleading. He did not move his hand to touch her, yet he could so easily have tried.

'You owe them nothing more,' he went on. 'You don't owe them your life.'

'Your liiiife . . . your liiiife!'

From inside the flat was a crash. Violetta started, and looked inside the bedroom. Something changed in her. She stiffened, then looked down. She let go with one hand. She was preparing to jump.

'Violetta,' pleaded Neil, 'don't let go. You owe them nothing now.'

'Oh, dear God,' gasped Felicity. 'Oh, dear God!'

Violetta let go, and began to fall, for an awful moment Felicity thought that she would crash down, but on that instant a white 'rope' snaked out and dropped over her head and shoulders, checking her. Hands appeared, clutching her. Scott leaned out above her, strong forearms and strong face vivid, clutching the billowing blouse, almost spanning her tiny waist. She began to struggle, but another pair of hands appeared, holding the 'rope' – Felicity could see now that this was made of knotted sheets. It was tight about her shoulders, too tight to allow her to wriggle free. Gradually, she was drawn through the window, long legs stretching straight out. Suddenly she was gone from sight.

Scott called: 'Half a jiff, Neil!'

Neil was still close to the wall with that finger and toe hold. Heavy beads of sweat showed where the light from the window fell on his forehead. Felicity thought he was trembling, too, quivering from the sustained physical effort. Very slowly he turned his head, the only part of his body that he could move with safety. When he looked sideways at her he was *smiling*.

'My day for taking chances,' he said.

Tears stung Felicity's eyes.

'Your day for being a hero.'

Scott appeared at the window again, leaning out, holding that rope of knotted sheets.

'Don't you move,' he urged, and leaned sideways to place the noose over Neil's head, over his shoulders. 'Rodeo,' Scott went on, 'London style. Can't exactly call it calf-catching, can you?

'... Left arm up, gently ...' He slipped the noose over Neil's arm, had it tightened securely about him, so that even if he slipped, he wouldn't fall. 'Now you can edge along,' Scott conceded. 'We've got two men on the other end of the rope, so not to worry.'

Neil let go of the ledge with his right hand, and leaned gently back against the rope. To this moment, the very end, he kept his head. Soon he was immediately beneath the window and Scott leaned out and gripped him beneath the arms. Neil used his knees and toes to help get up, and the moment came when he disappeared into the room.

Felicity said aloud: 'Thank God!'

Then she began to go dizzy, and nearly fell.

'Easy,' a man said behind her. He had a familiar voice, the voice of an American from the north: the voice of Randy Patton, old friend, old reliable. He took her by the shoulders and helped her down with arms nearly as strong as Pat's. She was trembling. 'It's all right, honey,' Patton said. 'It's all right.' He held her firmly, feeling her shoulders shake, and for a few moments she gave way, and sobbed; but the paroxysm was soon over, relief had brought reaction, that was all. She freed herself, and Patton held out a snowy white handkerchief. She blew her nose and then dabbed at her eyes. When she finished, and glanced up, Neil Commyns was coming into the kitchen, looking unbelievably immaculate. He came to a sudden stop when he saw Patton.

In a small voice, husky from tears and the tear gas, Felicity asked: 'Do you two know each other?'

There was a startled pause before Patton gave a short laugh and Neil chuckled, and suddenly both men were laughing as if at the greatest joke in the world. Felicity thought: There's nothing to laugh about, absolutely nothing, but she began to smile as she watched these two men. They were so different and yet there were marked similarities: Patton shorter, dark, handsome in a bold way, broad-shouldered and powerfully built; and Neil so tall and lean; hard-looking rather than powerful. Both were suffering from a sharp reaction after tension.

Scott came in, took one long look at each of the Americans, and then remarked:

'Someone once said that the English have no sense of humour. I begin to see what that means.'

Randy Patton managed to gasp: 'Nothing's funny?'

'Not to me,' Gordon Scott replied, cautiously.

'I'll go along with that,' declared Neil. 'It isn't funny. I'm sorry, Felicity. We do know each other.' He stifled a laugh, and something changed in him as it changed in Patton. He squared his shoulders, and his whole mood hardened. 'Salvatori, Pierre-Jacques and Lohn dead. What's been done, Gordon?'

'I'm assured that everything possible is being done at Rome Airport,' Scott answered.

'Which can mean something or nothing,' observed Patton.

'One thing is certain,' said Neil.

'What particular thing do you mean?'

'Salvatori and the others were killed because they were coming here with information,' Neil said.

'It's possible the killers were after someone else on board,' Patton pointed out, 'but I wouldn't vote for that.'

'It doesn't get my vote, either,' Neil put in, and they both looked at Gordon Scott.

'I'm going to assume the aircraft was blown up because the three police chiefs were on board,' Gordon said without hesitation. 'And I'm with Neil: they weren't killed simply to prevent us from having another conference, but because the Farenza believed the trio were bringing over some specific knowledge.'

Into the pause which followed, Felicity said very quietly:

'Such as, where Pat is being held?'

All of them turned towards her as if they had suddenly remembered her presence and were taken by surprise. It came to her that if that was the motive, then the Farenza almost certainly knew where Pat was; if they did his life wasn't worth the toss of a coin. Oh, Pat, Pat, Pat my darling! And it came to her that there might be another, much stronger motive for the cold-blooded crime; it was her life, her thoughts, which revolved only about Pat. Neil and Gordon did not speak, and by their silence seemed to agree with her fear. Out of the blue, Randy said:

'I shouldn't think that's the answer, Felicity.'

'Why not?' Neil demanded sharply.

'Because Salvatori told me how to find Pat,' stated Patton simply. 'So it's not a secret any longer.'

'Randy!' cried Felicity. 'Where is he? Is he safe? *Is he safe?*'

Neil Commyns watched Felicity, and had no doubt at all of one thing: she loved her husband. She might have affection, warmth, liking for him and for a hundred others, but Dawlish was her life. The truth of that showed in her eyes, echoed in her voice, revealed itself in the poise of her body. All that mattered to her was that her Pat should be safe. This was now in the forefront of his mind. Much else in the background; Violetta, soon to be questioned, for instance; and the motive for the destruction of the aircraft. The still unfathomed mystery of why this was all happening, also. But these things were set aside for a moment because of the love of a woman for a man.

All of these thoughts passed through his mind in a flash of time; there was little or no pause between Felicity's question and Patton's answer.

'Yes,' he said. 'He's as safe as a man can be.'

'Where?' cried Felicity.

'He is in a religious hospital somewhere in Rome,' Patton told her. 'Salvatori was afraid of another attack on him and asked for such sanctuary. He couldn't be safer than he is, and he ought to be left there until this case is over. The name of the hospital can be obtained only when the case is over, in fact. You can see that's wise, can't you?'

Felicity said, huskily: 'Yes, yes, of course.' In a breaking voice she went on: 'Oh, I don't know what's the matter with me tonight,' and hurried out of the room.

The men watched her go, making no comment, then turned back to one another. Neil moved, slowly, and led the way into the big room.

'I guess we could all do with a drink,' he said, and suddenly dropped on to the couch. 'Mine's Scotch on the rocks.' He looked very pale. 'So if Salvatori told you that and took such precautions, Randy, my idea is cock-eyed.'

'The idea that Salvatori might not have been reliable?' asked Scott.

'Sure.'

'Neil,' said Randy Patton. 'I've news for you.' He moved to the cabinet where the drinks were kept, obviously knowing the apartment well, and took out bottles and glasses. There were some nearly melted ice cubes in a bowl, and he salvaged some, poured the drink and carried it to Neil.

'Thanks,' Neil drank. 'What news?'

'Salvatori didn't trust you.'

Neil sat with the glass only an inch or two from his lips, but did not move.

'Is that right?'

'It's right,' Patton said. 'He called me and told me where Pat was. He said he hadn't told you because he wasn't sure of you. He wanted to know my opinion.' As he spoke, enunciating each word with great precision, Patton mixed two more drinks. He handed one to Gordon Scott, who said:

'Cheers.'

'Cheers.'

'Rah, rah, rah.' Neil sipped. 'And what did you say to Salvatori, Randy?'

Patton looked at him over the edge of his glass.

'I said I would trust you with my life.'

After a moment, Neil replied: 'Thanks.'

'You're welcome.'

'Did Salvatori happen to mention why he was coming? What particular piece of information he had to impart?' Scott asked. There was a touch of sarcasm in the question, as if he felt that the others were fencing. 'What would make it worth killing everyone on board an aircraft so as to silence three people?'

Patton answered: 'No. But he did say one thing.'

'What?'

'That the secret was in England.' Patton drank. 'What was found at the offices of the Celestia Travel Agency, Gordon? Do we know yet?'

'Yes,' answered Gordon Scott. 'All the addresses of Celestia Agencies throughout the world, a complete record of the staff of each agency, and an equally complete record of all the branches – seventy-two in all – of the Euro-Economique Transport Company which has its headquarters in Ghent, Belgium. I couldn't act for the Crime Haters but I could for Scotland Yard, and I had the A.C.'s approval to send a message to all the police forces where there is either a Celestia Agency or a Euro-Economique depot. Each is being closely watched.'

Patton finished his drink, then raised the empty glass to Scott.

'Who wants the rest of the world while we've still got Scotland Yard?' He put the glass on a table. 'I wonder if Violetta Casselli knows what it's all about. It's time we questioned her.' He rubbed his hands together very slowly, making a faint hissing noise, as he went on: 'I don't know why she's been handled with velvet gloves so far, but the time has come to show the iron hand. Too much is at stake to wait any longer and if we have to get rough, we'll get rough. Does anyone disagree?'

'I don't think you will have to,' Felicity said from the door.

Each man turned round, to see her with Violetta, and two Yard men close behind her.

CHAPTER EIGHTEEN

VIOLETTA SPEAKS

NEIL THOUGHT: She's astoundingly beautiful.

Randy wondered: Is she just a smooth liar?

Gordon Scott thought: I hope to God she's telling the truth.

As these thoughts and others passed through their minds, Violetta Casselli was speaking in her clear, pretty English. She had a little trouble with her 'r's, but no more than made her voice more attractive. She looked pale, but there were no shadows under her eyes and the pallor may have been due to powder; she wore neither rouge nor lipstick. She was not diffident because of the men, all accusing in their way, nor

135

apparently nervous of the fact that policemen stood just outside each door. She sat next to Felicity on the big couch, looking very demure.

She said, without evasion, that her family and all her
relatives were members of the Farenza. She explained what
they already knew; many of the members were called on to
serve the Farenza only once or twice in their lifetimes; few
who lived ordinary lives were expected to commit crimes of
any significance. They would pass on messages, hide individuals who were on the run from the police, hold parcels
without knowing what was in them. Many did not know that
the Farenza was a centuries old criminal organization; that its
leaders organized gangs and crime with near military
thoroughness; employed assassins, thieves, embezzlers,
forgers, perjurors. Moreover, it had sheltered behind the
Mafia for a very long time, and the Mafia was blamed for many
of its crimes. There was, she said, an inner ring of the leaders,
whom few if any knew. There was, close to these, the people
employed directly by the inner ring; and there was the vast
mass of the 'family', the innocent ones.

'But in time of need all could be used,' she stated. 'One
disobeyed only on pain of death; or forms of blackmail; or
threats to one's close friends and relatives.'

'So you know the Farenza is utterly ruthless,' Gordon Scott
said.

'Yes.'

'Yet you served it loyally,' Patton said, harshly.

'I am a member of it,' said Violetta simply. 'A member
should prefer death to betrayal.'

'Is that why you attempted to kill yourself?'

'Yes.'

'Who made you a member?' Patton demanded.

'My father, and my father's father,' she answered, and so
removed the need for further questions of that kind. She 'be-
longed'. She owed the Farenza her loyalty. For many years she
had worked for the Celestia Travel Agency, not only as an
interpreter but in a confidential position liaising between
London and Rome. She suspected that large sums of foreign
currency handled by the Agency's *Bureau de Change* were
stolen but had never asked questions.

'You knew you were handling stolen currency but did nothing,' Neil said, coldly.

'Yes,' Violetta answered. As she turned to look at him, her eyes seemed huge. 'It was my way of life.'

'You mean, you saw the Farenza as above the law,' Patton interposed.

'Not above it,' she answered. 'Apart from it, and also a law in itself.'

Patton raised his hands and dropped them helplessly to his sides.

'When did you become more deeply involved?' Neil asked.

Violetta turned and looked at Felicity, who rested a hand on her arm reassuringly. She was troubled for the first time, moistened her lips as she hesitated, and said at last:

'After Mr. Dawlish became interested in Mario Galli.'

'Your manager?'

'Yes.'

'Do you know Galli is under arrest?' asked Scott.

'No,' she said, slowly. 'No, but I am very surprised. He was so sure that he would get safely away.' Her eyes closed, as if this news was too heavy to bear, but she opened them again as Neil said:

'All those who are in danger of being captured should kill themselves.' When she made no comment, he went on: 'How do you know Dawlish was interested in Mario Galli?'

'He came to see him,' answered Violetta.

'Did he make accusations?'

'No, but he asked many questions which alarmed Mario, and which Mario reported to the head of the agency in Rome.'

'By telephone?' asked Neil.

'By cable, in code,' Violetta answered.

'And the reply?'

'That he must kill Dawlish,' she answered; and she shot a glance at Felicity, who simply closed her hand reassuringly round the other's forearm. 'I was to lure Dawlish into a trap.'

'And did you?'

'Three times,' Violetta answered, in a very thin voice.

'How?'

'We – we became friends,' Violetta answered.

137

'Close friends?' asked Patton, quietly.

'Yes.'

'*Lovers?*' demanded Neil. There was an edge to his voice, perhaps because he hated asking the question. He watched Violetta closely, so evading Felicity's gaze, but had he looked at her he would have seen that on Felicity's face was a secretive little smile, clearly of affection.

'No,' Violetta said. 'We were not lovers. Had he wished, we would have been.'

Now Felicity was smiling more broadly, but she did not speak.

'What did Dawlish want of you?'

'Information about the agency,' answered Violetta. 'And I gave him some which could do no harm, and allowed him to assume I was a traitor. I do not know whether he believed that. He was always prepared, that is why he escaped.' She closed her eyes again, as if to shut out a vision. 'I led him to a place where he was nearly killed by a car. Next I led him to a quiet street, where he was shot at. Also I stole the key to his car so that it could be stolen, made dangerous, and then returned to him without him knowing that it had been stolen.' Her eyes were tightly closed, now; and Felicity's hand was very firm about her arm. 'I tried to send him to his death. And now he is dead.'

The men caught their breath, as if on the same instant.

Felicity began: 'Must we keep up . . .?' but Neil cut across her words.

'You deliberately betrayed him three times, then.'

'Yes,' Violetta answered, almost inaudibly.

'Yet you told me you were in love with him.'

She said again: 'Yes. Yes, he came to mean very much to me.'

'Yet your loyalty to the Farenza means that you would betray him time and time again. That makes no sense.' Now Neil's voice was harsh in accusation. His lean, lined face was like the face of a judge, when the words ceased his mouth closed like a trap above his thrusting jaw.

Very slowly, Violetta said: 'Belonging to the Farenza is like belonging to a country. Which must one betray? One's self? One's beloved? Or one's country?'

She drew her hand free from Felicity's and covered her face with both her hands. For a few moments there was silence, which lasted until Neil's voice broke the quiet like a lash.

'Yet you are prepared to betray the Farenza now. Let us have the truth – you are as loyal to the Farenza as ever. You are pretending to tell us all you know to save your own skin, to fool us.' He went closer to her, one clenched hand thrust close to her face, his own body quivering as if with hatred as much as rage. 'Let's have the truth, *now*. What is the Farenza doing? What did Dawlish find out that is so dangerous? Tell me, here and now.'

Violetta opened her eyes but did not cower back. Her voice was stronger now than it had been when she had been talking of Dawlish.

'It has to do with robberies,' she said.

'What robberies?'

'That I do not know!'

'Don't lie to us! What robberies are being planned?'

'I cannot tell you because I do not know,' Violetta insisted. 'They were to be very big robberies. The agencies all over the world were to be used. That much I know because Mario Galli told me, but I know nothing more.' She looked steadily up into Neil's eyes and repeated: 'I know nothing more.'

Neil growled: 'I don't believe you.'

'The hell I don't believe her, either,' rasped Patton. 'Come on, you lying bitch, what's going on?'

'Let's have it,' Scott said harshly. 'You know.'

Felicity got up and went across the room and stood looking over the floodlit buildings and the river and the skyline of London shown vividly by the moon. There was nothing she could do; nothing she should try to do. Violetta might be lying. She did not think that was so, but it was possible. She, Felicity, believed that if the girl could admit to trying to lead Pat to his death, then she would not lie about anything else. Felicity clenched her teeth and held her hands stiffly by her sides. These men were her friends and each one had a special place in her affection and esteem, but they had a job to do. Even if it meant driving Violetta to desperation, even to the borders of insanity, they would do it.

Again the telephone bell blasted across the voices. 'Don't

lie.' *Burr-burr*. 'What are they planning?' *Burr-burr*. 'How many men have you sent to their death?' *Burr-burr*.

As if each realized that they would learn nothing more from Violetta at this moment, all three men turned towards the telephone. Randy Patton was nearest, and he lifted it and barked:

'Captain Patton here ... Who? ... *What? ...*' The sudden vehemence and the alarm in his voice affected them all, and Felicity moved towards him, hands raised in front of her breast, fearful as always that this was bad news of Pat. Patton was scowling more than looking shocked, and he went on: 'Sure, I'll tell him.' He put down the receiver, and looked at Gordon Scott. 'Mario Galli just poisoned himself,' he stated. 'He had cyanide inside a filling in one of his teeth. Apart from this woman, he was our only hope of finding out what's going on quickly.'

As one, they turned back to Violetta.

But this time Felicity went towards them, stepped behind the couch and placed her hands on Violetta's shoulders, both a defiant and a defensive gesture. Violetta had her hands pressed against her forehead, as if this new shock of Galli's death was more than she could bear.

'Felicity ...' Patton began in a stern voice.

'There's something you should know,' Felicity said, 'and this is the time for it. If I'd told you earlier it might have made it difficult for you to go on doing your job – especially you, Neil. Pat told me about his meetings with Violetta, but he gave me no details. He told me he knew she was in love with him yet kept on betraying him because of a prior loyalty. He said he was absolutely sure in his own mind that she couldn't tell him more than she had: that her employer knew what was going on but Violetta did not. She was too much in love with him to be a safe risk. I don't think Violetta can tell you more than she has. And it is even more vital for me to know than it is for you,' she went on in a clear voice. 'I can't live with Pat under constant threat from such an organization as this.'

When she stopped no one spoke for a long time. At last Violetta turned round and looked up, eased herself free from Felicity's hand and raised her own towards Felicity, in clear and deep appeal.

'I know nothing,' she said. 'I swear to you I have told you all I can.'

For a few minutes the three men talked together, and reached general agreement that Violetta had told the truth. Should they leave her here or take her to one of the nearest police stations? They decided to leave her, under strong guard, with Felicity. All three went out together a little after midnight. The Embankment nearby seemed thronged with policemen, and two cars preceded the one in which they travelled back to old New Scotland Yard and up to Dawlish's office there. Four men were on duty in the main office, and reports were coming in from all over the world. Sixty-eight of the seventy-two Celestia and allied agencies were closely watched, and eighty-one out of eighty-four Euro-Economique depots were as closely guarded.

Other reports had come in.

Salvatori himself had ordered a check of all the luggage on the aircraft; that had caused the delay, so it was certain that the bomb had been in the luggage of one of the police chiefs *or* one of the customs officers who had helped in the search had deliberately allowed it to go through. Each of the ground crew and customs men was being interrogated.

None of the prisoners in London had made a statement, and none was yet represented by a lawyer; it looked as if the Farenza had decided to sacrifice them. All would be up for a magistrates' court hearing in the morning.

Galli had quite openly prised out the stopping which concealed the cyanide capsule with a toothpick. A police sergeant and a police officer had been with him when he had bitten on the capsule; he had been dead within a minute in a cell which reeked of the odour of bitter almonds.

There was nothing at all to indicate where Dawlish had been hidden.

There was nothing to give any clearer indication of what the Farenza planned or for when the coup was planned.

'I know one thing,' Gordon Scott said. 'We all need a good night's sleep. Especially you, Neil.' He no longer had any diffidence about using Neil's first name. 'Mind if I make a suggestion?'

'Make any suggestion you like,' Neil invited.

'Take a sedative,' urged Scott, earnestly. He looked so boyish, so scrubbed and fresh-faced. 'You've done ten men's work today.'

'I shall take a bourbon on the rocks,' declared Neil. 'That is all the sleeping tablet I need.' He laughed, a little half-heartedly. It was true that he felt tired out and he probably looked it, but a sedative . . .

For half an hour he lay awake and began to think Scott had been right. All he could see were faces. Dawlish's, Felicity's, Violetta's. And young Scott, urging him to take a sedative. Slowly he sank into sleep, and the last visions he had were of Dawlish's face and then Felicity's, when she had looked both hopeful and despairing for her husband.

Neil thought: Where *is* Dawlish?

Then he slept.

As Neil Commyns slept, Dawlish stirred to waking.

There was a faint light; a low-powered electric bulb; and silence. He lay for some time, aware of light and silence and of himself, but slowly he began to think. To *think*. His mind was more alert than it had been in any of his previous awakenings; alert, and quite clear. Before he had wanted Felicity, but now he knew there was another reason, beyond his longing for her. She was the only person in the world whom he could trust; and she was surely the only person in the world whom his captors would allow him to see without suspecting his motive.

He said very softly but very clearly: 'I want to see my wife.'

From a corner where he could not see a man replied in a quiet voice:

'You must rest, my son. When you have rested you will be able to see her. But first you must rest.'

And the man he had not known was there went out.

CHAPTER NINETEEN

'MIRACLE'

REST, thought Dawlish, bitterly.

'Rest!' he muttered aloud, angrily.

'I'm sick of rest!' he said clearly and distinctly to the empty room.

He scowled up at the ceiling.

He was more aware of his head, his thoughts, his body, than he had been for an age. He had no idea how long he had been here or where he was, but was beginning to be sick of the inactivity; of being in shadows most of the time. Of course they were filling him with drugs, with painkillers, but just now he had no pain, only awareness of the fact that he was a prisoner, trapped, with no one whom he could trust nearby. No one. No one he could trust because there was no one he knew. How could one trust a little man who called him 'my son'? Why not 'old chap' or 'old fella', or 'my lad' or 'my man'?

If – if only he could get out of here.

There, across the room, was the door. The man had opened it at a touch and there had been no sound of a key turning in the lock when he had closed it; there had been just the soft click of it latching, hardly any sound at all.

So, it wasn't locked.

He eased himself up on his pillows, to see it better and to see the room better, not knowing that what had just come about had been a miracle. He was thinking mechanically; observing simple things and absorbing them without effort. True, he had done this all his life, even when at his first school; in those days, as for so many years since, he had observed and absorbed and then acted upon his knowledge, which had often seemed uncanny to others, who had accused him of acting on 'hunches'. For as long as he had lain here he had been unable to do this: his mind and his consciousness had been dulled. Now, he was nearer normal than he had been since he had been shot.

Shot.

He could remember so vividly how they had been fooled.

He had planned with great care, acutely aware of the danger. He had deliberately set out to draw an attack on himself, so that his assailants could be caught, and a lead found to the leaders of the Farenza.

Danger was in the very air.

Up the stone steps he went, one at a time, slowly, slowly, talking to Salvatori on the one side and Henri Pierre-Jacques on the other. He was certain he would be attacked.

But when?

Out of the blue, the shots, cries, alarm, thudding footsteps and fleeing men. It had happened exactly as he had expected, or had failed exactly as he had prayed. The danger all gone, all that mattered was to catch the men. One of the flower-sellers, a little woman, very attractive with bright eyes and olive-coloured skin and great shiny eyes, had seemed to proffer him a bunch of flowers. He could 'see' it at this moment as he lay in bed, still some way off. Dwarf roses, camellias, japonica, mimosa. He had been so relieved that he was still alive that he had put his hand in his pocket and paused. Others were watching, Salvatori's men, they could go after the assassins.

Some sixth sense had warned him.

He had even had time to move slightly to one side.

He had not actually seen the gun or the second assailant but above all other sounds he had heard a *zutt!*, had seen a flash on the perimeter of his vision, and then felt the impact. They'd prepared a second line of attack in case the first failed. *They'd got him*. With the understanding came a single spasm of fear, as if his whole body had been split asunder; then, oblivion.

Most of the time since there had been oblivion, but gradually periods of consciousness had come; of awareness. Each one was longer, each person seen and each emotion felt and each thought experienced with sharper awareness, until he felt almost himself again. And he remembered that a date was of vital importance. May the first. What day was it now? What day was it?

There was the door.

There was he, obsessed by this date: May the first. He did not know what was going to happen on that date but it was burned into his mind. May the first. May Day. Workers' Day.

What was to stop him getting out of bed, going to the door, peering out, escaping. He had experienced much worse than this, it would be easy. Easy! He needed only to talk to Felicity, whom he could trust. Not Salvatori or Pierre-Jacques or anyone else among the Crime Haters because he feared that one of them had betrayed him but he was not sure which one. He had to get out of bed; that was all.

He pushed back the bedclothes.

He was sweating, and a flush of heat surged over him; and a slashing pain went through his head. He cried out. The door opened and the man came rushing in, two nurses with stiff aprons and winged caps behind him. The man reached him before he fell back, saving him from banging his head on the iron bedstead. By that time he was unconscious again; in a deep, black void.

The sun was shining in at the top of a window when Neil Commyns woke. A maid was by the side of the bed, a tray in her hands, and on the tray was orange juice in a tall glass, and what looked like a pot of tea and a pot of coffee. Hugged beneath her right arm were the newspapers. She was middle-aged with frizzy grey hair, a high colour and a nice but nervous smile.

'It's ten o'clock, sir,' she said.

'As late as that!' exclaimed Neil, sitting up too suddenly; his head swam.

'Yes, sir. He told me to wake you at ten o'clock, but he wasn't sure if you'd like tea or coffee or orange juice, so I brought them all.'

'Why, thank you,' Neil said. 'Who told you to call me?'

'A Mr. Scott, sir. He said he would telephone at half past ten.'

'Did he come here?'

'Yes, sir, at nine o'clock,' she answered.

'That was very good of him.' Neil gave her a smile and she went out, closing the door with great care. He steadied, adjusted pillows and sipped orange juice, then opened the newspapers. The headline screamed:

Fire Bomb Outrage in Strand

There were pictures of smoke billowing and crowds surging. He scanned the text, which had nothing new to him, and turned the page. A two-column headline cried:

Shooting in Knightsbridge

And underneath this, a subheading:

Two Italians Arrested

There was nothing new in that, either; he scanned the outlines of world events – wars, revolutions, famines, an earthquake, rumours of wars, hi-jacking, strikes, youth protest marchers, cheek by jowl with sporting events, fashion shows, scandals, gossip. One single-column headline on an inside page read:

May Day Parade in Red Square, Moscow
(Moscow, April 29th)

This year's May Day Parade in Red Square will be the biggest ever, if reliable sources close to the Kremlin are right. Russia's biggest war-head, said to contain enough nuclear power to wipe out a city of five million souls, will be on show.

So will a hundred thousand of Russia's best troops.

A hundred thousand workers.

A hundred thousand children.

A thousand tanks.

Five hundred aircraft including 100 MIGs.

There is likely to be a single theme: Hate China. Western observers are convinced that the display of military might and national solidarity is for Red China's benefit: not the West's.

Whatever the reason, Red Square's May Day Parade is going to be the biggest and the most fearsome ever. Yet standing here in Red Square with the moon glowing on the onion-shaped spires of St. Basil's Cathedral and on the windows of GUM, the biggest department store in East or West, it is hard to envisage such a display of might. The moon manages to woo a gleam of reflected light from the cobbles, and a few dozen people are sauntering across the Square, discussing – of all things! – opera. They have just come out of the new opera house inside the Kremlin walls.

Tonight, May the first seems a year, not two days away.

Neil put the newspaper aside, finished the orange juice, discovered cold toast under some greaseproof paper, and butter on the side. Now the May Day Parade was only a day away: tomorrow. He had a quick shave with an electric razor and a shower, towelled vigorously, and dressed as he drank coffee and ate the cold toast. What was it about the English which thrived on being cold? He thought contrarily of air-conditioning and ice, laughed on a gruff note, began to let his mind roam about the Farenza problem.

What was being planned?

And when?

If there were any news of urgent importance, Scott wouldn't have given him so much time. He choked on a piece of toast, had nothing to wash it down with except the cold milk for the tea. He drank. It was half past ten by his watch, and Scott was likely to be on time.

The telephone by the bed rang, and he schooled himself to pick it up slowly and to say unhurriedly:

'Neil Commyns here.'

'Neil,' Gordon Scott said, 'There's the V.I.P. conference at Scotland Yard this morning at eleven o'clock. Can you make it? I can have a car outside your hotel in five minutes.'

'I'll be there,' Neil promised. 'Is there anything new?'

'Only panic in high places,' Scott replied laconically, and rang off.

Neil put down the receiver, had a quick bath, then asked for the number of Felicity's flat. 'I'll call you back,' the hotel operator promised, so he began to dress hurriedly, quick but economical movements. He felt fit, had no ill effects from his excesses of the previous day. As he dressed these all passed through his mind, in vivid scenes. The most vivid were the minutes when he had clung to the wall pleading with Violetta not to jump. Would she have jumped, anyhow? He felt sure she would, but that wasn't the key question. Why had *he* gone out of that window? Thinking back, he knew that it had been a kind of reflex action; if it came to that, so had Scott's, but Scott hadn't climbed right out.

Why had he?

One glance should have been enough to have told him he could do nothing, and yet he had not paused to consider, had just climbed out, crawled and pleaded. Had it been because Violetta was such a vital witness? Or had it been because he had not wanted her to die?

He had been following her for over a week; she had become almost an extension of himself.

What the hell was he thinking about?

As he roared the question inside his head the telephone bell rang; this would be his call to Felicity. Suddenly her voice sounded in his ear and he realized at once that it was high-pitched with excitement.

Earlier, when Felicity woke, she had the now familiar heavy-heartedness on waking, due entirely to fear for Pat. She lay snug and warm on her side, looking across at his pillow. They had a huge bed, called a king-size in America, with ample room for each to sleep soundly without disturbing the other. Now she was aware only that he was missing; aware that what she had keyed herself up to face ten days or so ago, could still become horribly true.

He might never come back.

'I must jerk myself out of this mood!' she exclaimed, and sprang out of bed, made tea, peeped into Violetta's room and saw that she was still fast asleep, looking so beautiful that Felicity could only pause to stare. Late last night, Felicity had told her the truth about Pat, had seen her great relief and sensed the new anxiety. She drank tea. Several letters were on the kitchen bar, so one of the policemen had brought them in. Most were from friends abroad and she was almost sure they would be condolences. She read the same newspaper as Neil was to read later, bathed, and then found Violetta wrapped in a towelling robe which was too big for her; it was primrose yellow. She looked almost too beautiful above the softening colour. They had breakfast of omelettes, toast and butter, Violetta preferring jam to marmalade. Gordon Scott called to say there was no news. Would there ever be any? For a few minutes despair swept over her, and she jumped up and went off into her own room, but she couldn't leave Violetta alone for long. She dressed in a loose-fitting shift dress, dark brown trimmed with gold, and went into the big room. Violetta wore the same blouse and skirt as she had yesterday. As Felicity went in she said:

'I am so very sorry there is no news.'

'I'm used to long periods of silence from Pat,' Felicity said.

'It must be a very difficult life to lead.'

'In some ways, very,' Felicity confessed. 'In other ways it's wonderful.'

'Fel – Felicity.' It was Violetta's first effort to pronounce the name, and it came out so prettily. 'I – I can remember how you feel, because he – he meant so very much to me.'

'Yes,' Felicity said. 'I think you do understand more than most.'

The telephone bell rang in the strangely companionable silence which followed.

There was no reason why this should not be an everyday kind of call from friend or relative, shopkeeper, or newspaperman – anyone. Yet Felicity stiffened and Violetta seemed to draw back within herself. The bell went on ringing. She moved across to the end of the couch and lifted the receiver.

'This is Mrs. Dawlish.'

'Good morning, Mrs. Dawlish,' a man said briskly. 'This is the Commercial Cable Company ... I have a cable for Mrs. Patrick Dawlish. That *is* you, isn't it?'

'Yes.' A cable; probably of condolence; conceivably, just conceivably, from Pat! But if he were able to send a telegram he was surely able to telephone in person. 'What does it say, please?'

The man answered: 'I shall read it slowly, Mrs. Dawlish.' Something in his voice warned her that he himself was excited, that this wasn't just routine. 'It is from Rome.'

'*Rome!*' she cried.

Violetta took a swift step forward.

'Yes, Mrs. Dawlish. And it says' – the man sounded as if he were breaking news to her, and why should anyone break good news? – 'your husband is making gradual improvement and now has periods of lucidity. Stop. In one such period tonight he called your name frequently and was clearly anxious to convey a message to you. The message was: *"Be careful, May the first."* That is all, just *"Be careful, May the first."* I regret I am not able to disclose my identity but you may rely on the veracity of this message. Wellwisher.'

Felicity heard every word, and yet they seemed to merge into one another. Relief, shock, bewilderment, all these emotions ran through her. Odd phrases were vivid in her mind. 'Gradual improvement . . . periods of lucidity . . . "Be careful, May the first".' Oh, dear God, he was not only alive but he was able to think! She didn't speak. Violetta took her arm. She sat down slowly. The man from the cable office spoke with alarm in his voice:

'Are you there, Mrs. Dawlish? Did you understand the message? . . . *Are you there?'*

A man said quietly: 'Yes, Mrs. Dawlish is here. I'm a police officer. If you will repeat the message I will write it down.'

'Right!' the cable clerk almost crowed. 'It must be wonderful news, but what a shock! The whole world thought that Dawlish was dead. It's from Rome and it reads . . .'

Felicity, knowing that one of Scott's men had picked up the extension, simply sat back, and closed her eyes. The realization of all it meant seeped slowly through her mind. It was ridiculous that tears should force their way between her lashes but they did. Violetta was crying too. What a couple they were!

She was almost herself again when Neil Commyns' call came, and she told him what she had learned.

CHAPTER TWENTY

V.I.P.s

NEIL entered the conference room on the fourth floor of the new New Scotland Yard at eleven o'clock precisely. Gordon Scott was standing at the far end of a long, horseshoe shaped table in a modern room without windows. At least twenty people were there, including Randy Patton and several of the police chiefs he had met in Rome – a Dutchman, a Dane and a German among them. At the head of the horseshoe was a grey-haired military-looking man whom he recognized from photographs as the Commissioner of London's Metropolitan Police. Neil took a chair indicated by a steward, and as he sat down, the Commissioner stood up.

'Good morning, gentlemen,' he began in a low-pitched but carrying voice. 'I am glad you were all able to come, and even more glad to have news of some significance.' There was a stirring among the men, a raising of heads, a tensing of expressions. 'Although a record is being kept of this meeting' – he glanced down at a youthful-looking man with a tape-recorder on a small table in front of him – 'what I have to say is for the moment highly confidential. There appears to be a most unexpected turn of events and an indication if not yet evidence that our colleague Deputy Assistant Commissioner Dawlish is not dead but alive.'

At first there was a stupefied silence.

As he watched their faces, the dawning wonder on the faces of men who had seemed so stern and reserved before, he realized how much Dawlish meant to them. He sensed the near veneration which he inspired in the middle-aged and in the old. Relief, joy, satisfaction, all showed vividly. The Commissioner waited just long enough, then read the mystery cable. After he had read it, copies were distributed together with several sheets of mimeographed papers, clipped together. The Commissioner went on:

'So we are warned that tomorrow, May the first, is the key day for whatever crime is being planned. The reports now in front of you summarize the results of the investigations so far made, and the precautions taken. It lists also the names of the men and women arrested, and you will see that apart from Violetta Casselli, no prisoner has made any statement of importance.' He paused, then continued: 'However, she has described the nature of the organization known as the Farenza very lucidly. And she appears to expect some exceptional scale of robberies. Other reports, not only from Mr. Dawlish but from police forces throughout the world now reveal the Mafia-like organization which has very wide and deep ramifications. It can rely on the loyalty of tens of thousands of people, perhaps hundreds of thousands of people. We know that its benevolent activities have concealed the fact that it is an international crime ring whioh indulges in most kinds of crime. We believe it has in the past smuggled drugs, currency, works of art and a great variety of objects through its transport arm, Euro-Economique. We can assume also that alongside the legal activities of this shipping company and of the travel agency – the Celestia – illegal activities have been widespread. We can be virtually certain that Mr. Dawlish did make a significant discovery, which the Farenza wanted to keep secret; hence their assassination attempts on Mr. Dawlish – which, if this morning's missive can be relied on, have happily failed.

'We may reasonably assume that the Farenza is planning a major coup.

'We have this message from Mr. Dawlish that it is to be staged tomorrow, May the first, a very significant day in many parts of the world.

'What we do not have,' went on the Commissioner, very earnestly, 'is any knowledge of the nature of the coup. One would not expect it to be political although of course that is not impossible.' He paused again and gave a sweeping glance around the table, his gaze resting on each one as if to convey an intensely personal message. 'I have invited you here in the hope that one or more of you may provide us with a clue as to the nature of what is planned. One clue might well be enough when men of your experience are able to bend your minds to it. I have called together as many of you as was practicable at such short notice, for we have very little time. In fact, we have a little over twelve hours until May the first, gentlemen; a little over twelve hours.'

He sat down, abruptly.

No one moved and no one spoke for what seemed a long while, until Otto Prenzler, of West Germany, rose stiffly from his chair. He was a man in the early forties with iron grey hair brushed upwards in a quiff.

'I wish to ask if we are wise to assume it is not political,' he said. 'In my country there will be some demonstrations tomorrow. In East Germany, many more. In Russia, perhaps, the most. But even here in England there will be some, and in the United States' – he glanced at Patton – 'there will be some also. In this political sphere, of the workers, the day is of such importance. Why not then for the Farenza?'

As he finished and sat down there were murmurs of approval: of 'Hear-hear', or 'That is sensible'. Neil Commyns could see the validity of the suggestion but felt a compulsive *no*. It was too obvious, and the Farenza was not a political organization in the real sense. There was probably a good reason for May the first being selected but it was not political.

An idea flashed into his mind. He half-rose, but Gordon Scott was on his feet already, a glint in his eyes which suggested that an idea had seized him, too. But he was very formal as he said:

'May I make a suggestion, Mr. Commissioner?'

'We shall welcome it,' the Commissioner said.

'Thank you,' murmured Gordon, and he moistened his lips. His nervousness showed in the precision with which he uttered each word. 'There will be these political demonstrations in all the big cities and many smaller ones. The police will be out in force to prevent outbreaks of fighting and rioting. If the Farenza plans a substantial coup in many places at the same time, a day when the police are already preoccupied in most of the world would be a good one.'

Someone called out: 'Of course!'

Neil thought with fierce exhilaration: That's it. My God, it's obvious!

'But what iss it to be?' a man cried out in broken English.

153

'If the success of the coup is going to depend on the police being too distracted to concentrate,' Scott said in a clear voice which sounded above all the others, 'it is likely to be by road. It if is going to be by road, it will be by car or truck or lorry. That can only mean the Compagnie Euro-Economique.'

A man roared: 'In Sweden, we must stop them!'

Neil thought in a helpless kind of way: He's already stopped them. He sent the requests out last night! Everyone here may not know it, but he's prevented whatever it is before it's really started! What a second-in-command!

The Commissioner was saying in a manner not far from blunt.

'Gentlemen, *please*.' The exclamations and the rustling of movement stopped as he went on: 'If you will refer to Sheet 3 of the reports in front of you, you will find that we felt justified in asking the police of all the nations where there are depots of the Compagnie Euro-Economique to have the company's transport vehicles watched, and only three of the authorities approached have not yet replied. Every vehicle and every depot of that company as well as every office of the Celestia Travel Agency anywhere in the world is being closely watched and guarded. I think it may be safe to assume that whatever is planned will fail to materialize. Precisely what is planned we have yet to find out, but it should not be difficult to exercise a little patience – for twenty-four hours, perhaps.'

Some of the delegates were laughing, most smiling, a few were doubtful and worried. The meeting began to break up, the foreign delegates starting out at once for their own countries to strengthen the watch on the depots and the agencies.

Nothing suspicious happened anywhere that day but in the early hours of May the first the big lorries of Compagnie Euro-Economique moved out of their depots everywhere in Europe and in the rest of the world. The police took no action but kept each under close surveillance. The big trucks parked close to entrances to main highways. Soon after ten o'clock next morning, cars and small vans drew up alongside the trucks, and boxes were taken on board. The police, still watching, compared notes by radio-telephone. In each city and each country the reports were the same.

Neil Commyns sat with Gordon Scott in Dawlish's office as reports came through.

Soon, there were variations in the reports: of thefts from diamond dealers and jewel shops, from druggists, from manufacturing chemists, from antique shops. Most of the thefts had taken place during the night, most had been cleverly camouflaged, and discovered late. By twelve noon, when most of the May Day parades had started and the police were preoccupied with crowd control, the Euro-Economique trucks were sealed by the drivers and drivers' mates, and the engines were started. The first actually to move was one from a side street off the Champs Élysées in Paris. Before it reached the corner, police were stationed all about it. The driver made a desperate effort to get away but was brought down by a *gendarme,* who took his keys from him and unlocked the truck.

Inside was a treasure trove . . .!

Gold and silver, copper and lead, bullion, treasury notes, jewellery, industrial diamonds and expensive drugs, furs, *objets d'art,* antiques, paintings, everything of value which could be stolen and taken to another country and sold with its value unimpaired, was stacked inside that truck.

Neil Commyns heard the report telephoned from Paris with fierce excitement; then one came from West Berlin, another one from Stockholm, another from Madrid, yet another from Rome. The reports came in too frequently for Neil to comprehend in detail, but the staggering fact was that the Farenza had planned robberies on stupendous scale, and the trucks of the Compagnie Euro-Economique had been ready to take the loot across national borders to big cities. Soon it was apparent that the goods would have been stored in the depots and then slowly released on the market. The Celestia agencies would take the bullion and currency notes, acting as bankers and keeping small consignments of precious stones and drugs in strong-rooms and safes.

Some trucks were allowed to reach their destination before being held and searched. Drivers, goaded by their fears, began to talk. Managers of the Celestia agencies were questioned and in most cases arrested, for already they had in their possession smuggled currency and stolen gold.

All over Europe hundreds of arrests were made. Many, too, in the big cities of the United States, in fact in all the world. What had been planned as the largest scale crime in history proved to be the biggest fiasco known. The police cells were jammed full, the leads back to the organizers grew clearer ...

'The truth is,' Neil Commyns said to Felicity and Violetta late that afternoon, 'we've not really reached the heart of the Farenza. The leaders have burned their fingers badly and it may have put them back years, but it will be a long time before we catch them all.'

'Will that matter so much?' asked Felicity. 'Now they've suffered such a crushing defeat they won't be able to do much for a very long time.'

'You mean you want to hold everything in abeyance until Pat can put them all out of business,' Neil said dryly. 'I wonder where the devil Pat is.' He moved across the big room and took up the stance that was so like Dawlish's; and the others joined him, one on either side. He put his arms round their waists and they made a curiously affectionate picture as they watched London's skyline. And he felt remarkably at home.

There was a ring at the front door.

Neil gave each waist a squeeze, then turned and went to the passage. No police were on guard inside, now, and he hoped that was safe. He opened the door an inch, to see Gordon Scott, and even before Scott was inside, the eager brightness of his eyes betrayed his excitement.

He held a small black brief case under his arm. One corner was burned, and in one side a jagged tear.

'Hallo,' he said. 'I think I've some news.'

He went into the big room ahead of Neil, who saw Felicity's face light up. But she didn't speak. Scott held the brief case out, and placed it on the arm of the big couch. By now, Neil could see that it was badly damaged, and suddenly the truth dawned on him. But he did not spoil Scott's pleasure.

'Guess what that is,' Scott said, and answered the questions before they could begin to. 'It is a fireproof brief case found in the wreckage of the Boeing from Rome. It is General Salvatori's. And ...' He opened it, showing that it had been unlocked when he had arrived, and drew out a letter. 'Addressed to you,' he went on, and gave the letter to Felicity.

She held her breath. It was a long time before she could bring herself to open it, but at last she tore it across one corner and slit it along the top edge. Her fingers were unsteady as she took it out. Violetta stood between the two men, watching her fearfully, lest the news was bad.

But the light in Felicity's eyes was suddenly like flame.

'Pat is in the private hospital at the Vatican!' she cried. 'Salvatori arranged with Cardinal Gasperi to have him looked after there. And they were under oath to tell no one without his permission. Oh, thank God, thank God!' She spun round towards the hallway. 'I must go to Rome. I mustn't lose a minute. Gordon, please check the flights, there *must* be one tonight. Violetta, please make some sandwiches, everyone must be famished! Neil, do see if anyone wants a drink.' She rushed out as if blazing a trail, clutching the letter to her bosom.

'Salvatori not only didn't trust me, he didn't trust anyone,' Neil said, as he sipped a Scotch on the rocks. 'Except the priests!'

'I don't blame him,' Gordon Scott said. 'You know that the recording which Pat had made disappeared. And' – he tapped the brief case – 'there's another letter here, to me. He says that the Farenza discovered where Pat had been sent to after the operation; there was an attempt to wreck the ambulance he was moved in; *so someone betrayed that.* Salvatori decided to say nothing to anybody after he asked for sanctuary at the Vatican. He wrote these letters and sent copies by mail, and brought these himself. It's almost as if he knew he might be speaking from the dead.'

Neil nodded. Violetta crossed herself, and held his arm tightly. Soon, Scott was on the telephone. There was a non-stop flight to Rome at a quarter to nine, Felicity had just time to catch it.

'Felicity!' he called. 'You've just twenty-five minutes!' He got on to the Yard, to arrange for an escort, and soon he was driving Felicity to the airport, and Neil was talking with Violetta, who could stay here at least until Felicity came back.

'Neil!' she said. 'What will the police do with me?'

'They won't take any action,' Neil Commyns said quietly. 'The British have a system called Queen's Evidence, which is like our State's Evidence. If you tell them all you know in court, you will have nothing to fear. I am sure, honey – as sure as I can be.'

She was very still; grave, demure-looking, and quite remarkably beautiful. He felt his heart miss a beat, and began to realize what was happening to him. He placed his hand on hers. She looked at him intently for a moment, and then smiled.

Five hours later and a thousand miles away, Dawlish came out of sedation for the second time that day. Facing him was one of the nursing sisters of an order he did not know. She was young, fresh-faced and pretty. He had the sense not to move suddenly as he asked:

'Do you speak English, nurse?'

'I should do,' she answered. 'I am English.'

'Thanks be for that!' he said. 'I've been trying for days to make someone understand that I want to see my wife. I . . .' He broke off, caught his breath, and then went on as if in pain: 'What – what day is it?'

'May the second,' she answered, and he groaned. But as he groaned he heard a movement from the corner at his side, and he turned round – and saw Felicity. A great joy surged through him, but even as she ran towards him, he said hoarsely:

'Fel darling, the Farenza was going to stage a worldwide robbery yesterday, using Euro-Economique trucks. It can be disastrous, the biggest robbery ever known, it . . .'

'Darling,' Felicity said, 'all the robberies took place. So far there have been two hundred arrests and over a hundred million pounds' worth of stolen goods have been recovered, thanks to . . .'

She didn't finish.

He was holding his arms wide, and his strength was such that even in his weakness he could hold her tightly.

THE END

CALL FOR THE BARON BY JOHN CREASEY,

writing as Anthony Morton, creator of The Baron

A series of minor thefts at Vere House prompts Martin and Diana
Vere to call in their old friend John Mannering to investigate. But
while Mannering is doing so, the jewels and the famous Deverall
necklace belonging to Lady Usk, a guest of the Vere's are stolen.
Reluctantly, the police are brought in and much to Mannering's
disquiet, Scotland Yard send their top man, Chief Inspector
Bristow, one of the few who suspect Mannering to be the Baron –
the cleverest jewel thief in the country.

And Mannering realizes it is even more imperative that he
prove his innocence when he discovers someone has planted the
stolen Deverall necklace in his room . . .

552 09297 5   30p

DEATH IN HIGH PLACES BY JOHN CREASEY,

writing as Gordon Ashe

Capt. Patrick Dawlish is on manoeuvres in the wilds of Salisbury
downs when he receives a cryptic message from Colonel Cranton
to meet him next day in Salisbury. Once there, he finds his old
friends Tim Jeremy, Ted Beresford and his fiancee Felicity, have
also been summoned – but no-one knows why.

Then, just as Colonel Cranton arrives, his car is involved in a
strange accident that Dawlish realizes was deliberate and in which
the Colonel has been seriously injured. Leaping into another car
he sets off on a dangerous chase that is to lead him through a maze
of murder, espionage and blackmail before he is able to crack the
riddle of Colonel Cranton's message – and the organization behind
it all . . .

552 09286 X   30p

A SELECTED LIST OF CRIME STORIES FOR YOUR READING PLEASURE

All these books are available at your bookshop or newsagent: or can be ordered direct from the publisher. Just tick the titles you want and fill in the form below.

CORGI BOOKS, Cash Sales Department, P.O. Box 11, Falmouth, Cornwall.

Please send cheque or postal order. No currency, and allow 10p per book to cover the cost of postage and packing (plus 5p each for additional copies).

NAME (block letters)...

ADDRESS...

....

(APRIL 75) ....

While every effort is made to keep prices low, it is sometimes necessary to increase prices at short notice. Corgi Books reserve the right to show new retail prices on covers which may differ from those previously advertised in the text or elsewhere.